PICTURE ME SEXY

Rhonda Nelson

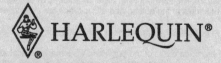

HARLEQUIN®

TORONTO • NEW YORK • LONDON
AMSTERDAM • PARIS • SYDNEY • HAMBURG
STOCKHOLM • ATHENS • TOKYO • MILAN • MADRID
PRAGUE • WARSAW • BUDAPEST • AUCKLAND

ISBN 0-373-79119-4

PICTURE ME SEXY

In this world, there are men and there are heroes.
And if a woman is lucky, she'll wind up with the latter—
a man who will love, protect, guard and defend her
at all costs, who will be her best friend and more,
a great partner, a great father. My brother-in-law,
Tracy Vanderford, is one of these men—a true hero.
I'm so thankful that he's there for my sister and niece.

You're a special person, Tracy.
I'm so glad you're part of my family.

Prologue

MEMPHIS LINGERIE QUEEN Delaney Walker jilted—again!

Delaney muttered a soft oath as she stared grimly at the newspaper. Given the state of the economy, the scandal with the Catholic Church, and the recent war, one would think that the *River City Herald* could feature something besides her pitiful social life on their front page. It was ridiculous really. Journalism and the state of society was at an all time low if her busted love life was considered news. Hell, it wasn't news, Delaney amended—it was entertainment. She grimaced.

She was entertainment.

The moment she'd gone from being a struggling designer to an overnight success, Delaney had become Memphis's bad-girl icon. Never mind that the moniker didn't fit, that the reputation was a complete figment of society's imagination. She designed hot, racy lingerie, ergo she must be hot and racy. Her lips curled wryly.

Ha. Nothing could be further from the truth.

That mentality coupled with her penchant for dating the occasional baseball star and for her alarming tendency to get engaged and—just as quickly *un*-engaged—didn't help matters in the least. Memphis journalists followed her every move with avid interest, got paid to print her humiliations as if her life were merely the next chapter of a running joke. Most of the time, Delaney didn't care. Any publicity was good publicity as far as she was concerned. She'd always fumed about it in private, then laughed all the way to the bank.

But for reasons she didn't understand, it was harder to summon the laughter this time, and even harder to laugh her way to the bank.

Delaney suspected that glum realization stemmed from the fact that Roger worked at the bank.

Her spineless ex hadn't even had the common courtesy of calling off their engagement in person—he'd taken the hi-tech approach and e-mailed her. That had been a first. She'd been dumped over dinner and over the phone, but this was the first time she'd been given the old heave-ho via the information superhighway.

But it would be the last. She was absolutely, unequivocally finished with men.

Delaney read through the article, winced at the accompanying picture. Hogsville. She looked huge. She was no dainty miss by any stretch of the imagination—she'd been an overweight child and still suffered the effects of that mentality—but in all fairness, the photo wasn't an accurate depiction of her true self. Her lips curled. If that were the case, then

Roger would have scales and a long forked tongue, which more accurately matched his character.

"Delaney...I have bad news."

Delaney looked up from her desk and met the worried gaze of her personal assistant. She blew out a breath and slouched back into her leather executive chair. "I've already seen the paper, Beth. You can lose the gloom-and-doom expression. Honestly, I'm surprised that they hadn't gotten wind of it before now." She and Roger had been officially un-engaged for almost a week now. Clearly someone at the *Herald* was losing their touch. The last time she'd been jilted, it only taken a couple of days for the story to break.

Beth shook her head, winced. "It's not that."

Delaney hummed under her breath. Interesting. "Am I going to need a Kiss or the Big Block?" she asked, using her own personal uh-oh scale. Amazing how many things could be gauged by chocolate. Some problems could be handled with a mere satisfying Kiss of chocolate. Others—like being dumped for the second time—required a larger dose. That's where the Big Block came in. She'd consumed quite a bit of chocolate over the past week—the only food weakness she'd allowed herself to keep once she'd finally carved the pounds off she'd hauled around as a child—but she'd vowed to get her addiction under control. Amazing what a new attitude could do.

Beth bit her bottom lip. "Definitely a Big Block."

Uh-oh, Delaney thought. That didn't bode well for

her peace of mind or her hips. Thank God for anti-depressants and Lycra, she thought with a droll smile.

With a silent sigh, Delaney tossed her pencil aside and donned a friendly expression despite the familiar sensation of dread swelling in her belly. She'd detected a flash of pity in Beth's tense gaze and instinctively knew that this particular morsel of bad news wasn't business related—it was personal.

The worst kind.

Nevertheless, Roger had already called off their engagement. Whatever Beth had to tell her couldn't possibly be any more humiliating than that.

Delaney pulled in a bolstering breath, plucked a block of chocolate from her drawer and sat it on her desk. Still, it couldn't hurt to be prepared. "Well?"

"You know that trip to the Greek Isles you wanted me to cancel?"

Delaney snorted and rolled her eyes at her assistant's attempt at tact. "You mean my honeymoon?"

"Er…that would be the one, yes."

The one that she'd spent months planning, that she'd insisted on paying for herself because her dream honeymoon had been so exorbitantly expensive she'd felt guilty asking Roger's proud but poor parents to foot the bill. Roger, the tightfisted bastard, had never offered to share the cost with her. *Thrifty,* she'd rationalized. *A good money manager.* He'd routinely stuck her with bills that he should have paid all under the guise of not "infringing upon her independent nature.'' What a jerk. Delaney mentally tsked and shook her head. How plainly she could see that now.

''What about it?'' Delaney finally asked.

Beth shifted miserably. ''I, uh, can't cancel it.''

Delaney blinked, taken aback. ''What? Why? I know that it's last minute, but I still should be able to get a partial refund.'' Roger's cousin owned a local travel agency and had pulled the honeymoon together for them. Considering she'd been the injured party in the breakup, she never expected any problem in canceling the trip and recouping part of her funds. In order to avoid further humiliation, she'd given Beth the job of calling. She should have known she wouldn't be so lucky. ''Get them on the phone,'' she sighed. ''I'll take care of it.''

''Believe me,'' Beth sighed wearily. ''If it was that simple I wouldn't be in here.''

''But it is simple,'' Delaney insisted as an insistent quiver of annoying alarm vibrated in her belly. ''I've paid for a honeymoon package that I no longer need—being as I'm no longer going on a honeymoon,'' she added pointedly.

Beth chewed her bottom lip. ''You might not be going on a honeymoon…but Roger is.''

The room dimmed and brightened all in the same instant. The bravado inspired by her new I-hate-men-because-they're-faithless-disloyal-oversexed-unprincipled-bastards attitude momentarily wavered. ''I'm sorry?''

With a sympathetic sigh of regret, Beth made her way across the plush rose carpet and lowered herself into one of the red satin wingback chairs that fronted Delaney's huge antique desk. She swallowed nervously. "Roger and his, uh, new bride are presently on their way to Greece."

So she'd been wrong, Delaney thought numbly. Being dumped for the second time just short of the altar *wasn't* the most humiliating thing that could happen to her—being dumped, summarily replaced, and having your dream honeymoon *stolen* from you was much worse.

Curiously, the idea of Roger having married another woman didn't bother her nearly as much as the stolen honeymoon. A significant revelation lurked in that thought, but Delaney was too upset at present to ponder it. Honestly, would this nightmare ever end? The papers would undoubtedly have a field day with this latest twist in the Delaney Walker saga. Being a local celebrity of sorts was great for sales, but hell on her personal life.

"Well." Delaney forced a bright smile and envisioned herself serenely denuding Roger's prized antique roses. Revenge therapy played a significant role in her new attitude. "Just exactly when did the happy couple depart?"

"This morning," Beth said gravely. "Roger called and asked the travel agent to bump everything up and issue new tickets for his new...for Wendy. Sorry. Yours were nonrefundable."

Wendy the accounting wonder, Delaney realized with a spurt of undue surprise. Obviously during all of those late-night meetings, Roger had been checking out more than the bottom line of his personal finances—he'd been checking out Wendy's as well. Delaney ignored the prick of mortification this newest disgrace brought and blew out a disgusted breath. Well, wasn't that just par for the course? Clearly the temptation of a cost-effective honeymoon—after all, it was hard to beat *free,* Delaney thought darkly— was too much for them to pass up.

The familiar burn of anger and humiliation roiled through her stomach, flashed up her neck and scalded her cheeks. She instinctively tore into the Big Block, broke off a piece of chocolate and popped it into her mouth. Good grief, she'd thought she'd worked past this. After this last fiasco, she'd taken a good hard look at herself and had decided an attitude adjustment was in order.

With the previous jilting, Delaney had taken the brokenhearted, but proud and dignified approach. She'd laughed when she wanted to cry, she'd been calm when she wanted to scream and she'd never— *never*—acted anything less than respectable. She'd always tried to be the bigger person, and what had it gotten her?

Dumped again.

She'd been left with another mess to clean up. Had Roger considered canceling the caterers? No. Helped with returning gifts? Uh-uh. Delaney once again mourned the loss of her china, the beautiful Wedgwood *Floral Tapestry* she'd planned to display in the gorgeous antique china cabinet her grandmother had left her. No, Delaney thought as irritation knotted her insides, Roger hadn't planned to see to anything. And really, in all fairness, why would he? She'd always been the perfect little fiancée. Too well-mannered and polite to do otherwise. He'd fully expected her to do it.

Because she'd always been a sweet Memphis belle, Delaney thought with no small amount of self-disgust.

Because she was a respected businesswoman with ties to the community.

Because, while she might design some of the most sensual, most erotic lingerie in the business, he'd known that she'd *never* had the gumption to wear it, much less do any of the wicked, depraved things in the bedroom her creations implied or inspired. Roger, the two-timing, self-serving spineless weasel had known her secret, had known that she was so miserably modest that she'd only do it *at night, in the dark,* and *under the sheets.*

Her phobic modesty had been a bone of contention between her and Roger, particularly in the bedroom. But Delaney simply couldn't help the way she felt. No matter how much weight she lost, no matter what size she finally shrunk herself into, when she looked in the mirror, she still saw the fat, ridiculed child she'd been. No matter how unreasonable it seemed, how bizarre, she couldn't seem to work past it.

Still, as a way of proving that she could learn to be adventurous, could learn to be the sexy siren he so desperately wanted, Delaney had decided to give Roger boudoir photos as a wedding gift. The shoot was scheduled for this afternoon. At first, she'd planned to cancel it, but upon further consideration, had decided that the first step in becoming a new woman meant getting past old issues. What better place to start than with her modesty?

While she could have had any one of her photographers here at *Laney's Chifferobe*—her catalogue lingerie business—do the spread, Delaney had booked an outside business to handle her photos. There were some things that were simply too personal to share with people she saw on a day-to-day basis and required anonymity. Despite present circumstances, her lips curled into a droll grin.

Boudoir photos of the boss certainly qualified.

The photographers employed by *Laney's Chifferobe* were accustomed to peering through their lenses and pulling lollipop perfection—stick-thin bodies with big heads—into focus. Delaney's size ten pear-shaped body didn't fit the bill. Not just no, but hell no. She'd clean up roadkill before she'd offer her less than perfect form up to that kind of critical scrutiny. She'd had enough of it as a child to make up for a lifetime.

Delaney knew that Roger planned to come back

from his honeymoon and find the mess of their broken engagement cleaned up, expected to waltz back into River City Bank and continue to manage her company's account, and he fully expected her to be the bigger person—translate *doormat*—she'd always been.

Well, he expected wrong, and would be in for a rude awakening when he and darling Wendy returned.

Once the initial hurt and humiliation had worn off, Delaney had taken a long critical look at herself and decided a change was in order. She'd spent too much of her time trying to be perfect, had wasted too much of her time on men. She was a two-time loser in the game of love. Clearly, her radar was faulty, otherwise she'd have been able to find a faithful one by now, one that hadn't had an ulterior motive—like soliciting her business. Her last three serious relationships had shared that same common denominator—in one capacity or another, they'd all stood to benefit from her business.

No more.

She'd tried, she'd failed. The end. She'd decided a married happily-ever-after simply wasn't in her cards. At least with a man. Women by nature were more faithful creatures. Though she knew it was doubtful—she'd always been fascinated with the opposite sex—Delaney had decided to broaden her scope. In an effort to spark some latent lesbian tendencies, she'd begun listening to Melissa Etheridge, had started watching re-runs of *Ellen* and *Rosie*. So far no luck, but who knew? She grinned. The right woman might come along and trip her trigger.

To be quite honest, everything that was feminine and maternal had rebelled at the idea of giving up on love—she desperately wanted a family of her own—but she'd reached a point where there was simply no other alternative. A change was in order. Since men seemed to be the problem, she'd simply take them out of the equation.

In the new world according to Delaney Walker, all men sucked.

Her eyes narrowed. And Roger, in particular, sucked. Irritation bubbled through her veins, triggering a finger twitch. It seemed that revenge therapy was in order again.

"Delaney, are you all right?" Beth asked tentatively. "Do you need me to do anything else for you?"

Delaney nodded succinctly. "As a matter of fact, I do. Clear my schedule for the rest of the week and get me a gallon of weed killer."

Beth's eyes widened in confusion. "Weed killer? In winter?"

"That's right," Delaney told her, warming to her plan. She really enjoyed this form of therapy. It was very cathartic. "And make sure that it has a spray nozzle."

1

ARMED WITH A GALLON OF fast-acting Weed-Be-Gone and a pair of garden gloves, Delaney wheeled out of the parking lot of her downtown Memphis office and aimed her sporty sedan toward Germantown, the posh upscale neighborhood Roger—the ball-less worm—called home.

While her sorry ex could squeeze thirteen cents out of every dime, there were a couple of areas in which he simply didn't spare any expense—his home and his lawn. Roger was a master gardener who spent every free minute and every spare penny landscaping his award-winning lawn. He was particularly proud of his turf, an expensive evergreen designer blend that stayed bright and lush even through the harsh winter months.

The word "asshole" written in dead grass would contrast nicely, Delaney thought with vengeful glee.

She pulled into the drive, made quick work with the weed-killer and just as quickly made her escape. The rush of adrenaline triggered a burst of giddy laughter, pushed past the irritation and made her feel absolutely wicked.

Delaney loved feeling wicked. She got the same

thrilling rush from designing her lingerie. There was something so intensely satisfying about creating an outfit that inspired such an intimate, sensual act. One she'd spent an inordinate amount of time fantasizing about. Being an overweight child, then overweight teen, had definitely been to her advantage in one way—the lonely hours had inspired her creativity, had essentially led her into her career. She wanted the women who wore her lingerie to feel sexy in it, empowered. Wanted them to revel in their sexuality, their femininity.

Speaking of empowered, who would have ever thought that such an asinine prank would be so satisfying? So mentally beneficial? She chewed her bottom lip and vaguely toyed with the notion of snatching a few of his prized antique roses, but quickly dismissed the idea. She didn't mind resorting to a little vandalism to smooth her ruffled feathers, but she wasn't quite brave enough to become a thief…yet.

Besides, she had an appointment to keep. Granted, no one but she and the photographer would ever see her boudoir photos—but she wanted them anyway, knew she needed to take that first step toward progress. Delaney felt sexy while designing the clothes, but couldn't feel sexy in them because she'd always been so pathetically modest. That had to change. She needed to get past it, needed to garner a little of that feminine energy for herself.

She pulled her car into a parking space designated

for Martelli Photography, grabbed her garment bag from the back seat and mentally prepared herself to battle her modesty. Her stomach knotted. She'd find happiness in little victories, she decided as she made her way into the old building. Why? Because men sucked.

The scent of fresh paint hit her the moment she stepped into the old building. She nodded to a couple of workers and ducked under a scaffold in order to reach the antique cagelike elevator. The old Gloria Gaynor song "I Will Survive" played a continuous loop in her head, bringing a smile to her lips and a bounce to her step.

Delaney grinned, pleased with the rush of endorphins this whole new men-suck philosophy had given her. She began to chant it aloud softly—verbal reinforcement—and listened to the words echo as the ancient elevator slowly lifted her to the top floor.

"Men suck, men suck, men suck." Damn, that felt good, she thought. So good that, since she was alone, she upped the volume and added a little more U.S. Marine *oomph!* to the suck part. "Men *suck,* men *suck,* men *suck.*"

A deep masculine chuckle reached Delaney's ears about the same time that a pair of manly bare feet came into her line of vision. As the elevator slowly drew up into what was obviously a penthouse suite, a pair of long denim-clad legs gave way to an extremely impressive bulge centered between a set of impossibly narrow hips. Blue cotton clung to a washboard abdomen, perfectly sculpted pecs and widened into a pair of the most beautifully muscled shoulders she'd ever had the pleasure to pant over.

The man was built like a brick wall, which seemed appropriate, considering she felt like she'd just run into one.

Dark brown wavy hair, a tad too long to be fashionable, framed a sinfully handsome face that attested to pure dumb luck and good Italian genes. His lips were a fraction overfull for a man and presently curled into one of the laziest, sexiest grins she'd ever seen. Dark brown eyes, heavy-lidded beneath slanted brows, glinted with humor, old-soul intelligence, and the promise of unnamed pleasures. Everything about him exuded confidence and strength, and pure sexual heat rolled off him in waves. He was sex with a capital S and to her immeasurable astonishment, she wanted him instantly.

Really wanted him.

The breath stuttered out of her lungs in a whoosh of longing, her womb clenched, her nipples tightened and her very bones seemed to melt beneath the heat of no-holds-barred raw, primal desire.

Mr. Sex anchored one hand at his waist and held a camera loosely in the other. He had great hands, big and tanned with blunt-tipped fingers. You could tell a lot about a man by his hands, Delaney thought absently.

"Men suck, eh?" he asked in a voice that was

smooth and deep and sang in her ears like a soulful jazz tune.

Delaney moistened her suddenly dry lips, managed a nod. Yes, they did…and mercy she'd just bet this one would be great at it.

SAM HAD ENVISIONED his first meeting with the legendary lingerie queen Delaney Walker as many things, but he could honestly say that hearing her cheerfully chant "men suck" in that sweet southern drawl as the elevator lifted her up to his loft apartment/studio and then having her stare at him as though he were one of those chocolate bars she purportedly loved to eat, was not one of them.

Sam was accustomed to garnering female interest—he was a Martelli after all, and, among other curious phenomena, his family had never lacked general sex appeal.

But something about the heat in Delaney Walker's bright green eyes was different from what he typically encountered, went beyond lust, beyond desire. He couldn't put his finger on it exactly, but it made his scalp tight, his skin prickle and, curiously, the very air around him seemed to change as she blinked out of her lust-trance and breezed past him into his loft.

His gut clenched with trepidation as a thought suddenly occurred to him, but he dismissed it as ludicrous. This bizarre feeling couldn't possibly be what he suspected.

It could not.

Even if Sam had any intention of ever marrying and starting a family—which he most assuredly did not—he didn't believe in the "quickening"—the supposed almost supernatural ability for a Martelli to choose his mate. According to family history—and the testament of his various cousins, uncles, brothers and father—all of whom had never strayed and never divorced—a Martelli man simply *knew* when he'd found the one woman he was supposed to spend his life with. Supposed physical symptoms included gooseflesh, tingling skin and a sense of déjà vu…much like he'd just experienced, Sam realized with mounting disquiet.

Nah, Sam told himself, refusing to even consider the idea. He'd made the decision to remain single years ago, when he'd watched his father mourn his mother until the man was only a shadow of his former self. When he'd watched his brothers—big tough, rough, gruff men—become hopelessly besotted fools over their wives, watched them actually cry when their children were born. The idea of losing that kind of control over himself and surrendering said control to another person completely unnerved him. Sam grimaced.

He'd pass, thank you very much.

Clearly some melodramatic Romeo lurked in the Martelli family tree and had passed the story down from one generation to the next. Sam mentally harrumphed. If there was one thing an Italian loved more than a good marinara, it was a good story. Men simply fell in love and, to preserve the family tradition, called it a "quickening."

Sheesh.

As for fidelity and divorce being non-existent—the most damning evidence to contradict his theory, particularly in this day and age of the quickie divorce—that too could be easily explained. No brag, just fact, but Martelli men were smart. They were loyal, had a strong sense of family. Particularly his. Case in point, his family met for lunch every day at his father's house and woe be to he who didn't show up. His father expected them to be there and so far, regardless of how inconvenient, Sam nor his brothers had ever missed the mandatory meal.

Sam told himself that his peculiar reaction to Delaney Walker was only his overwrought imagination. Just a product of nerves. He'd hyped this meeting up in his head for the past couple of months, had been obsessing over it ever since she'd first called and scheduled her appointment.

Frankly, when the tabloids had reported that she'd been jilted again—bless her heart, the woman didn't seem to be able to get one to actually say "I do"—Sam had fully expected her to call and cancel the appointment. Curiously, she hadn't. And he'd never been one to look a gift horse in the mouth.

Sam's portfolio had been sitting in limbo at *Laney's Chifferobe* for months now and this meeting offered him the prime opportunity to showcase his talent and possibly secure a job with her company.

Sam loved women. Skinny, fat, short, tall and all species in between. There was something so intrinsically beautiful about the female form. All that soft skin, those gentle swells and valleys, the intriguing curve of a womanly hip, a silky thigh, a well-rounded rump. Women were utterly gorgeous and their bodies had always held a particularly keen fascination for him.

He'd never understand them, of course—what man in his right mind would even try? Everyone knew they were the most fickle creatures God ever created. But he loved them all the same and he had a real knack for capturing them on film.

With luck, Delaney Walker would see that.

Sam enjoyed doing the boudoir photos and the occasional wedding. It helped pay the bills, after all, and supported his rummage sale and estate habit. But ever since *Laney's Chifferobe* had hit the lingerie scene, he'd been itching to get a shot at it.

Delaney designed every piece of clothing and personally oversaw the layout of each issue, a monumental job in and of itself. She was a slave to detail and would settle for nothing less than total perfection. He had to give her credit, she was one helluva hard worker. She'd built the company from the ground up and hadn't simply hired someone else to oversee the details when she'd finally gotten the business operating comfortably in the black. No doubt about it, she had character.

But given that drive for perfection, that keen eye, why on earth did she settle for mediocre photography? It baffled him. The spreads lacked finesse, were almost clinical and not the least bit compelling. Honestly, why even bother with temperamental models? Why not just lay it all out and do still shots? The effect would be the same.

She didn't know it yet, but she needed him, Sam thought determinedly. Given the chance, with her creative ability and his expertise, they could make her catalogue sizzle.

And speaking of sizzle…Delaney Walker was hot.

Sam's artist eye quickly roved over her lush Marilyn Monroe body, summarized her finer features. She was small, generously curved in all the right places. She actually had hips, Sam noticed, pleasantly surprised. These days most women starved them off. She had a smooth heart-shaped face, a perfect cupid's-bow mouth, a dainty chin, bright green eyes, and long hair the color of moonbeams that hung like a silky curtain down to the middle of her back. Anticipation spiked. He couldn't wait to look at her through his lens.

That curious tingling gripped him again, made the fine hairs on his arms stand on end, and the familiar tug of reciprocated attraction gave a particularly vicious yank. Sam scowled, ruthlessly tamped it down, and made a conscious effort to get back to business.

Honestly, gawking at her while she absently roamed around admiring his loft was hardly professional.

"I see you brought your own bag," Sam said. "How many outfits will you be changing into?"

The graceful line of her back tensed and she pushed a shaky hand through her hair. "Three. Is that too many?" she asked hastily. "Because I can forego a couple of them. I don't have to—"

Sam chuckled reassuringly. "Three's fine. I just wondered how many settings we'll need to line up. We'll change backgrounds with each one. Any nudes?" he asked casually. Would that he would be so lucky. The rogue thought flitted through his mind before he could check it. Dammit, he had to get control of himself. He couldn't afford to be attracted to her. Wouldn't allow it.

Her eyes widened and a flash of outright panic momentarily lit up that bright green gaze. "Er, no."

Sam mentally frowned and his senses went on heightened alert. With the exception of few, most women who came to him were nervous about putting their bodies on display. They worried about thick thighs, small breasts and that extra ten pounds they'd put on since childbirth. Things that simply didn't matter to a man who loved them.

Men were visual. That's why they looked at *Playboy* magazines, watched the occasional flick, and liked to make love with the lights on. Men liked sexy and naked and, quite frankly, the immediate impulse of the combined two didn't leave time to log any imperfections. When a man saw a naked woman, the head with the brain instantly ceded control to the head without one. Men were animals. They'd been divinely wired to be fruitful and multiply. 'Nuff said.

Delaney Walker designed some of the hottest, sexiest lingerie on the market. She was a true sensualist. He would have thought that she, of all people, wouldn't suffer any insecurities about her body. Yet clearly she did, Sam decided as he studied her more closely. What an intriguing paradox. She obviously didn't have the balls-to-the-wall, wild-child personality her designs—or the local paparazzi reports—implied. He filed it away for future consideration.

"This is a fantastic place you've got here," she said. She'd strolled to the bank of floor-to-ceiling paned-glass windows and gazed at the old downtown Memphis skyline. "Did you do all the renovations yourself?"

"Most of them," Sam replied. "I did the majority of the cosmetic work, the painting and the floors, but I contracted out the plumbing and rewiring." He shrugged, rubbed the back of his neck. "I apologize for the mess the building is in. When the owner saw how well my loft turned out, he decided to renovate the entire building." Sam offered her a smile. "Things are chaotic right now, but it'll be nice when the work is completed."

She turned to face him and that sense of déjà vu slammed into him once more. She nodded succinctly. "Without a doubt. Your loft is lovely."

Irritated with his reaction to her, Sam redoubled his efforts to remain professional and merely nodded. *You've got a lot riding on this, Martelli,* Sam told himself. *Don't screw it up.* "So, are you ready to get started?"

She didn't look ready, Sam noted. In fact, she looked miserable. Indecision vibrated off her tight frame and she tortured that full bottom lip with her teeth. But just when he thought she'd decided against the session, she turned, pulled in a bolstering breath, then smiled and said, "Not ready…but determined."

He could see that, Sam thought, unreasonably impressed. Delaney Walker had moxie, a trait Sam found both equally attractive and appealing. He nodded, pleased. "Good. If you'll follow me, Ms. Walker—"

She snorted indelicately. "Call me Delaney. You're about to see me half-naked. I hardly think we need to stand on formality."

Sam felt his lips slide into a grin. "Fine. Delaney, it is then. I'm Sam, by the way. The dressing room is down the hall, first door on the left. Go change and don't forget."

She quirked a brow and her lips tucked into the shadow of a smile. "Forget what?"

Sam winked at her. "Men suck."

2
___

Delaney made her way down the hall he had indicated and felt her muscles marginally relax. She'd needed that bracing thought and decided that, in addition to being one of the sexiest creatures God had ever thought about putting on this earth, clearly Sam Martelli was intuitive as well.

Undoubtedly he'd read about her recent humiliation in the paper, but rather than bringing it up, or embarrassing her by trying to comfort her, he'd instinctively known just what to say. She hoped he carried that keen perception into the studio with him, because she was going to need every single ounce of determination to get through this shoot. Just the idea of putting on some of the outfits she'd brought with her made her entire body clench with dread. Made her throat dry and her palms itch.

But those weaknesses made her every bit as determined to see this through. She stiffened. She would do this shoot. She would wear her lingerie. She *could* and she *would*. For reasons she couldn't explain, she'd attached a tremendous amount of importance to conquering her modesty, to making this personal area of her life work. A new attitude without the actions to back it up was worthless.

Delaney found the dressing room and quietly let herself inside. The room was relatively small, but homey. An Oriental rug covered the dark hardwood floors. A small Duncan Phyfe sofa sat against one wall and a huge, heavily carved mahogany cheval mirror stood in the corner.

Rather than line the wall with hooks for hanging clothes, Sam had attached antique glass doorknobs. The novel idea drew a delighted smile. He'd done a phenomenal job blending the old with the new, and the resulting effect was warm and homey, yet eclectic and very romantic. She couldn't fault his taste and found herself genuinely intrigued by him. She suspected he was an estate sale/antique mall junkie like herself. Delaney's antebellum home was stuffed to the rafters with her finds as well. She couldn't drive past a junk store, yard sale, or antique mall without stopping.

She briefly wondered if a Mrs. Martelli were in the picture, but instinctively knew that wasn't the case. Of course, it could simply be wishful thinking on her part.

Irritation surged, which was ridiculous since she'd just recently decided to swear off men and possibly change her sexual preference. Honestly, what was wrong with her? She'd been given irrefutable proof—repeatedly—that men sucked. So what if he was possibly the sexiest man she'd ever seen? So what if her nipples still tingled and she still felt the residual heat of that flash fire her body had undergone the moment she laid eyes on him? So what if her wayward sex still throbbed and the moisture hadn't fully returned to her mouth? Other parts of her anatomy were astonishingly wet.

Delaney angrily jerked off her clothes, slung them over the couch and ripped into her bag. She snagged a white cotton peasant gown pulled it over her head and donned the coordinating thong.

She was 0 for 2, dammit. She couldn't trust her own judgment when it came to men. Any man. Even that one, though it pained her to admit it. She didn't need to be wondering whether Mr. Sex out there had a wife or not. All she needed to concern herself with was whether or not he could take a good picture. If his reputation held true, then she should be pleased.

Delaney turned, caught sight of herself in the mirror and wilted like a cheap corsage. Every ounce of self-deprecating anger drained out of her as she stared miserably at the image displayed in the mirror. It was a lovely gown, trimmed with French lace and tiny satin ribbon and she'd even reluctantly admit that it looked lovely on her. The cut was loose, with blousy sleeves, and it hung to mid-thigh. Very romantic. The gown was so utterly feminine, so sweetly sexy, it would flatter any woman.

Still, just knowing that she wore nothing underneath but a pair of thonged panties and her birthday suit was enough to send her heart rate into an irregular rhythm. The familiar weight of dread coalesced in her tummy. She shoved her hands through her hair, watched the long tresses fall over her breasts. Another defense mechanism, Delaney thought, disgusted.

Covering her body with clothes wasn't enough—she used her hair as well.

Oh, hell. Changing herself in theory sounded great, but could she pull it off in fact, as well? She bit her lip. Could she do this? Could she really do this?

A knock at the door startled her. "Delaney?" Sam called hesitantly. "You about ready in there?"

No, she wasn't ready by any stretch of the imagination...but like she'd told him, she was determined. Delaney pulled in a shuddering breath. "Yeah, coming right out."

She squared her shoulders, opened the door and met Sam in the hall. Something about his tall, reassuring presence made her feel marginally better. He briefly appraised her outfit, but his gaze didn't linger on any particular area. She didn't know whether to be thankful or perturbed, and decided not to ponder the conundrum while half-naked in the hall.

"The peasant gown." He nodded. "Nice choice. Follow me. The studio is this way."

Delaney did as she was told and followed him down the hall. The corridor dead-ended into a huge open area. Where the other end of the loft had been partitioned by walls to make living quarters, this end was one big, spectacular room with lots of space and light.

Several backdrops and props were sectioned along the walls. A bedroom scene, featuring a gorgeous king-size canopied bed with coordinating pieces. A sitting room scene with a beautiful French Rococo style chaise lounge. A bathroom scene, with an antique slipper tub, and another still that featured a gold low-backed sofa and various animal prints.

Sam didn't simply stop at getting the primary items to accentuate a scene—he saw to the details as well. Everything was rich with color and contrast, with candlelight, lamps, rugs and coordinating accessories. But most importantly, it was sexy and compelling. A thrill raced through her. She wanted to lie on that bed, that chaise, that couch, wanted to sink into that tub.

He'd obviously put a lot of thought, time and money into building this studio, Delaney thought, suitably impressed. In fact, his home studio looked considerably better than the few meager sets she had down at the *Chifferobe*. Visions of her models in this studio, decked out in various *Laney* creations began to traipse through her head.

"Is there any particular setting that draws you?" Sam asked in that smooth blues voice.

She laughed, shook her head and gestured to the room at large. "All of them do. This is incredible," she said appreciatively. "Really incredible. Did you do this all yourself, or hire a decorator?" She knew the answer before she asked the question—the entire loft had the same sensually cohesive feel about it—but wanted to be sure anyway.

He toyed with his camera and shook his head. "No decorator. My tastes tend to run to the eclectic." He looked up at her and smiled, which resulted in a serious quiver below her navel. To her immeasurable chagrin, heat bolted up her spine. "I don't think a decorator would get it."

Well, she most definitely got it and she loved it, recognized him as a kindred spirit of sorts. Her sensuality came through in her designs, his came through in his photography and decorating.

How refreshing to meet a man who seemed to take genuine pleasure and interest in surrounding himself with nice things. Even Roger—who'd possessed a great deal more class than most of the men of her acquaintance—had deferred to a decorator's judgment when furnishing his house. If he hadn't, the expensive Georgian home would undoubtedly be decorated with Elvis on velvet and bizarre sculptures made out of beer tabs.

"You've done a wonderful job," Delaney finally told him. "It's truly remarkable. Enough old and new to make it interesting."

"I like antiques. They have character." He took one last cursory glance at his camera, deemed it ready and looked up. "So where do you want to start?" he asked again, clearly ready to set this shoot in motion. "I don't mean to rush you, but we're losing natural light."

Delaney nodded. "Right. I, uh…" She looked from scene to scene, and tried to make her up mind. She bit her bottom lip. "Well, with this gown, I think the chaise would work best. But I'm not the photographer. What do you think?"

"I agree. The peasant gown has a whimsical feel. It'll look good against the green fabric on the chaise."

She wouldn't look good on the chaise, but the gown would. Delaney ignored the prick of irritation and summoned a smile. She didn't necessarily want him to find her attractive, still… She was half-naked and he was a man—he was supposed to notice.

While his unimpressed attitude certainly wasn't doing her self-esteem any good, she could truthfully admit that the familiar claw of desperation brought on by her modesty wasn't rearing its ugly head. She supposed there was nothing to be modest about if a man wasn't interested.

"I'm going to put on a little mood music before we get started," Sam said. "Do you mind?"

Still unreasonably perturbed, Delaney shook her head. "Not at all. Go ahead." Whatever tripped his trigger. Evidently it wasn't her. Which was good, Delaney reminded herself again and resisted the urge to grind her teeth. Men were a no-no. Right? Right.

Nevertheless, she found her gaze inexplicably drawn to him. She liked the way he moved, unhurried yet purposeful. Sensual. If the man paid such close attention to detail when it came to his home and his profession, one could reasonably deduce that he'd be an equally meticulous lover. Slow and thorough, leisurely—

Otis Redding's "Sittin' On The Dock Of The Bay" suddenly resonated from hidden speakers, derailing that unproductive line of thought. That smooth, smoky voice moved over her, pushed her lips into a late-blooming smile. Somehow the music choice suited Sam Martelli. He looked like the type who would appreciate Otis. He was a favorite of hers as well.

Sam tested the light around the chaise, and after a few adjustments, deemed it acceptable. "Okay. I'm ready when you are."

Delaney made her way over to the set, acutely aware once more of how little she wore. So what if it had long sleeves and hit her just barely below mid-thigh? What difference did it make if she felt naked?

"I was right," Sam said matter-of-factly. "The gown is perfect."

Delaney felt her eyes narrow as another wave of annoyance surged through her. The gown again. Not her. She was proud of the damned gown—she'd designed it, after all—but honestly. Wasn't it his job to make her feel sexy?

She expelled a frustrated breath. "Where do you want me?"

Two beats passed as he tweaked his camera again

and when he answered his voice sounded a little strained. "Why don't you lie on the chaise? Pick a comfortable position. A pose that's natural to you."

Delay arranged herself on the couch, propped her head up with her hand and curled her legs up close to her bottom. It was comfortable, but she didn't feel remotely sexy. In fact, she felt ridiculous.

Sam looked at her through his lens, then pulled the camera away from his face. A line knitted his brow. "Is there something wrong?"

"I, uh, don't feel sexy," Delaney confessed. "I feel stupid."

His lips curled into a lopsided grin. "You don't look stupid."

"I don't look sexy either."

Sam rubbed the back of his neck and winced. "Wrong, you *look* sexy, but you don't *feel* sexy and the two are hopelessly intertwined. I could try to remedy how you feel, but you're the most miserably modest woman I've ever seen and I'm not sure that what I could do for you would help. Any compliments I might give you would be genuine, but they're going to make you self-conscious. If you start worrying about what you're wearing—or not wearing—and how you look, then that's pretty much going to defeat the purpose. You don't have to look like a sex kitten, Delaney," he said patiently. "All you have to do is smile. Okay?"

He was right. She was being ridiculous. "Okay."

"Great." Sam's face disappeared behind the camera once more and Delaney conjured the smile he'd asked for. "So, who are these pictures for, anyway?"

Delaney smothered a grunt and rolled her eyes. "My next lover."

"Next?"

Delaney continued to smile, though she couldn't contain the edge to her voice. "Right. I'm sure you read the papers. My ex-fiancé and his new wife are currently on their way to Greece on a honeymoon that I paid for."

Seemingly astonished, Sam lowered the camera. "You've got to be kidding."

She snorted. "I wish."

"Damn, that's cold. What a bastard." Sam refocused, took a couple more shots.

"My sentiments exactly."

He moved to the left a couple of feet, went down on one knee and fired off a few more shots. "It's guys like him that give men a bad rap."

"I know. That's why I'm finished with them." Delaney rolled over onto her back and crossed her legs. Strangely, talking to him made her feel less ridiculous and she began to marginally relax.

"With men?"

"Yep." She twirled a strand of hair around her finger.

"So where does the next lover come in?" he asked, sounding faintly amused. Apparently he'd drawn the incorrect conclusion that she wasn't serious. Evidently he thought she was simply the typical thwarted female making the typical empty threat to swear off men. Wrong. She was an adult woman who'd made a valid, life-altering decision.

She should probably enlighten him.

Delaney curled back onto her side and smiled wickedly. For the first time since they'd started this shoot, she actually felt sexy. She arched an innocent brow. "Who said that lover would be a man?"

The camera clattered to the floor and the blank slack-jawed look he gave her was utterly priceless.

Delaney sat up and made a moue of disappointment. "Damn, that would have been a good shot. You missed it, didn't you?"

3

HE'D DROPPED HIS damned camera.

Never in the history of his career had Sam ever dropped his camera. When he went into the zone, the equipment simply became an extension of himself. His camera was his baby and he treated it as such— with extreme care.

No doubt about it, over the course of the past few years he'd been routinely shocked. He'd taken boudoir photos of a hermaphrodite, for pity's sake. Pictures of women that were pierced in areas that went well beyond his scope of comprehension. He inwardly shuddered. In this business, he'd pretty much seen it all and he'd never—*never*—once dropped his camera.

And yet, all this woman had to do was utter a few choice words about possibly changing her sexual preference…and he'd fumbled a thirty-five-hundred-dollar camera like a freshman rookie a yard from the end zone.

He couldn't believe it. He simply couldn't believe it. A litany of inventive curses streamed through his overwrought mind as he bent over and snagged his camera from the floor.

From the very first moment he'd laid eyes on Delaney Walker he'd known she'd be trouble with a capital T. For reasons which escaped him now, he'd thought he'd be safe once he'd gotten her behind the lens—thought he'd be able to treat her just like any other beautiful woman who came into his studio. And there'd been plenty.

In this line of business, any photographer worth his salt, in a sense, had to become desensitized to the female form. Battling a hard-on throughout a session was inconvenient and not conducive to a good shoot. One simply learned how to detach and focus on what lay inside the lens. Sam had mastered the trick years ago, and yet from the very second Delaney stepped out of that dressing room, his loins had been locked in a fiery state of perpetual hell. His blood had been humming with an intense awareness akin to radio static, and his scalp had tingled until he wondered if he might be having some sort of allergic reaction to his shampoo.

He was a wreck.

He didn't just want her—the driving need gnashing around inside him couldn't be reduced to any such simple term—*he had to have her*. Felt like he'd explode, or worse, if he didn't.

One look at her in that virginal peasant gown— hell, she might as well be in a nun's habit for all the skin revealed—and something deep, dark and primal had taken over. The hint of curves beneath all those yards of fabric, combined with that sexy mouth and long moonbeam hair and… Sam pulled in a tight breath. She was gorgeous, utterly gorgeous, and the fact that she didn't realize it made her all the more appealing.

He'd wanted to tell her many times during the first few frames just how incredible she looked, how phenomenally hot, but given her almost phobic modesty, he didn't think it wise. For his peace of mind, or hers. He'd tried to loosen her up with conversation and the ploy had worked right up until she'd dropped her little I-might-take-a-lesbian-lover bomb.

She had to be one of the most sexually innate creatures he'd ever encountered. She'd let that bright green gaze leisurely roam from one end of this body to the other, had all but measured him for a wet suit, yet she'd suddenly decided to bat for the other team? he thought skeptically. Not likely. He smothered a snort. If she was a lesbian, then he was the damned Easter Bunny.

Delaney's soft chuckle drew him from his chaotic musings. "I've shocked you."

"Not shocked," Sam said simply for the sake of argument. "Just surprised. I had no idea that you were a lesbian." He smiled up at her and tried to project a calmness he didn't feel. "I'd understood that your fiancé was a man."

He checked his camera over once more, deemed it unharmed, and once again tried to put things back on an even keel. Maybe if he concentrated really hard, he'd be able to think about something besides the way her gown had slipped down on her arm, baring one delectable shoulder. Besides tunneling underneath acres of white cotton and exploring every inch of her gorgeous body.

With his mouth.

"My fiancé was a man," Delaney told him, "as was the last one. Men suck. Why not give a woman a shot?" she asked matter-of-factly. "I can be open-minded."

Sam tsked, lined up another frame. "I don't think being open-minded has anything to do with it."

Delaney rolled over onto her stomach, let her hair fall over the end of the chaise. "Why not?"

He fired off another few shots, then paused. "Let me ask you something. Are you, or have you ever been attracted to a woman?"

She pulled a thoughtful face and winced. "No," she said slowly. "But I'm hoping I can work past that."

A laugh stuttered out of his chest. "That's certainly an interesting goal."

She pulled an offhanded shrug, baring a little more creamy skin. "Hey, a girl's gotta do what a girl's gotta do."

Sam finished off the roll of film. "Okay, that's got this set completed. Wanna go change and meet me back in here?"

He'd said it casually, hoping not to lose what little ground they seemed to have gained during this stage of the shoot, but the instant his suggestion registered, her anxiety returned full force. Previously relaxed muscles went tight with tension and a frown wrinkled the smooth line of her brow.

Sam pretended to tweak his camera and eventually she nodded. "Sure. I'll, uh, be right back."

Theoretically speaking, if he were an outlet and she a plug, then one could reasonably assume that when she walked out of the room—pulled the plug, so to speak—he would return to normal. The clawing need would subside, his mega hard-on would wilt, and his skin would quit prickling.

To Sam's disquiet, it didn't and he grimly suspected that until he had her, it never would.

And having her was absolutely out of the question.

Number one, he didn't sleep with clients. He'd worked hard to build a reputable business, depended heavily on word-of-mouth advertising. Everybody knew hell hath no fury like a woman scorned. One pissed-off chick with a vicious tongue could literally cost him thousands of dollars. Sam had seen it happen before.

Secondly, even if he were to forget the no-fornicating-with-a-client rule, it certainly wouldn't be with a woman as emotionally wrecked as Delaney Walker. Sheesh. She'd just been jilted, was so messed up that she was considering becoming a lesbian. He'd have to be the biggest fool on earth to even consider letting something become of this hellish attraction that had blazed between them.

Finally, were those reasons not enough—which

they certainly were—he desperately wanted a job at the *Chifferobe*. Wanted a shot at it so badly that he could taste it. This was his chance, dammit. He couldn't afford to screw it up by acting on an almost overwhelming attraction. He could handle it. Would have to.

With that bracing thought, Sam turned as Delaney tentatively made her way back into the studio. His mind blanked as every ounce of blood he possessed raced back toward his groin. Every hair on his body stood on end and his breath froze in his lungs.

This gown was a long, sheer black silk wonder that left her shoulders bare beneath spaghetti straps, snugged against the full mounds of her breasts, showcased a mere slip of a waist and the generous curves of her hips. Open eyelet work trimmed with red appliqued roses formed a slinky *S* that curled provocatively around one breast, over her abdomen, down her hip and finally landed at the floor-length hem.

Other than her arms and shoulders, and a few peekaboo places down the front, she was covered from head to toe, but as far as Sam was concerned she might as well be naked. All that silky light-blond hair lay pooled over one shoulder and she'd tortured that full bottom lip until only a trace of her lipstick remained. He had never in his life seen a more beautiful woman.

Never.

In addition to all of the weird physical sensations

he'd been subjected to since the moment he laid eyes on her, another more disconcerting feeling suddenly commenced in his chest, making it hard for him to draw a breath. It grew tight, then swelled with some unnamed emotion.

Delaney smiled self-consciously, making her all the more gorgeous. "Okay," she sighed. "Now where do you want me?"

His tenuous grasp on control almost snapped. *Where did he want her?* Anywhere. Right there. Who cared? The only thing that lay between him and her were about ten feet of hardwood and a couple of scraps of clothing. With a little creative maneuvering, he could take her right there. In a heartbeat.

Sam rubbed the back of his neck, forced the erection-provoking vision to subside. "What about over there?" He pointed to the animal print set. At the moment, he didn't trust himself to say more.

Delaney crossed her arms over her chest, inadvertently plumping her generous breasts even more, and moved to the set he'd indicated. She sat stiffly on the couch. "Okay. Now what?"

"Why don't you tell me about something that relaxes you?" Sam suggested, trying to loosen her up again. The tactic had worked before and perhaps a little conversation would make him quit thinking about tracing that peekaboo lace with his tongue. About bending her over the end of that couch and plunging into her sweet, slick heat from behind.

She forced a smile. Looked nervously around the room. "Chocolate relaxes me."

He chuckled. So those rumors were true. He'd heard of her legendary chocoholism as well as a couple of interesting tidbits about her office. He'd heard that her inner sanctum was crammed full of antiques, was decorated in shades red, rose and pale pink and had been designed to look like the inside of a jewelry box. He couldn't satisfy his curiosity about the one, but he could the other.

"Any particular kind of chocolate?" he asked as he lined up a spectacular shot.

"No, just plain unadulterated chocolate. No nuts, no caramel, no nougat." She grinned and arched a brow. "Just chocolate."

Sam took the shot and instinctively knew this frame would be his favorite. That gently curved, innocently provocative smile combined with the come-hither brow was awesome. With effort, he swallowed. "That was a gorgeous shot."

"Really?"

"Really. Tell me about something else that relaxes you."

She gave him another cheeky grin. "Sorry, don't know you well enough."

Sam fired off a few more frames. Despite the whopping erection swelling out of his briefs, he'd finally hit the zone, wanted to keep the momentum. "Forget that you don't know me. I'm getting some great stuff here."

She tsked. "I'd hate for you to drop your camera again."

Irritation rose. *Click, click.* "I won't drop my camera again. Move to the other end of the couch."

Delaney swung her legs around and did as she was told. Her breasts plumped against the arm of the couch. "Well, if you're sure…"

"I'm sure." *Click, click, click.*

She arched her back and a long stretch of leg peeked from a slit up the side of the gown. Another wicked grin played at the corners of her lips and her gaze once more made a slow head-to-toe inspection of his body. "Well, in that case…nothing relaxes me more than good hard orgasm…but those are really too few and too far between to be dependable. Not like chocolate. It always satisfies me."

Sam stilled. A bead of sweat abruptly broke out on his upper lip and if he hadn't caught himself, his camera most likely would have tumbled to the floor again. He'd expected her to tell him she liked to cross-stitch, or cuddle up with a good book.

She laughed out loud, a delighted chuckle that bubbled up her throat and hit a chord deep inside him. "Wow. I did it again. I shocked you." She sounded so damned pleased with herself, it was all Sam could do not to laugh.

He grinned, felt a blush actually creep into his cheeks. He ducked his head and passed a hand slowly over his face. "Yes, you did."

"I can't believe I said that," she marveled, suddenly embarrassed. Her cheeks pinkened adorably. "I'm sorry if I embarrassed you. I've done a lot of things lately that have been totally out of character."

"Well, save them for the next set," Sam told her. "I've run out of film again. You've got one more outfit, right?"

Still smiling, she seemed lost in her own private thoughts. "Yeah, one more. I'll be right back."

One more. Thank God. Then she would leave and he wouldn't have to worry about the "quickening"…or possibly ruining his perfectly good reputation for being a professional—or possibly his future—by sleeping with her.

If this torture session didn't end soon, Sam didn't know whether he'd be able to control himself. He'd been battling his exaggerated hormones for the past hour, and frankly he was beginning to suspect that this was simply a war he couldn't win. But it was one he knew he couldn't afford to lose.

DELANEY CHANGED INTO the final outfit, a blush satin baby doll teddy, as quickly as possible and didn't allow herself the luxury of looking in the mirror. Her modesty would rear its ugly head again and she'd lose every bit of ground she'd managed to gain during this experience. She was still self-conscious of her body, but nothing like the claustrophobic sensation of dread that she usually suffered from.

Sam had kept her talking so much that she'd barely had time to notice what she was or wasn't wearing. He'd drawn her out, made her say things that she'd never dreamed would come out of her mouth. Mortification burned her cheeks. *An orgasm relaxed her?* Where on earth had that come from? What had made her say that? Obviously, she'd tapped into some sort of repressed alter ego when she'd decided to embrace her feelings instead of re-pressing them. When she'd undergone an attitude ad-justment.

And really, why not? What difference did what she said to this man make? Her dirty laundry had been aired to all and sundry for the past several years. What could she honestly say that would embarrass her anymore than what had already happened to her? When she looked at it that way, it was really rather liberating, Delaney decided with a small smile.

Besides, after today, she'd never see Sam Martelli again. The thought struck an odd pang of regret, but she squelched it determinedly. She could have him mail the photos to her. There would be absolutely no harm or repercussions for anything she did or said. She'd sworn off men, so what possible problem could arise out of a little harmless flirtation? Beyond today, what difference would it make?

None.

She'd use this inconvenient attraction for him to her advantage. Shocking him made her feel sexy and looking at him turned her on. The man was art in motion. He moved with a predator's grace, with an economy of motion. Those heavy-lidded deep brown eyes had a way of making a woman wonder about hidden talents, about tangled sheets and satisfying orgasms. Delaney bit her bottom lip as a chord of longing vibrated deep in her belly. She'd just bet he'd be chocolate-covered sex, the kind she'd regrettably never had.

Oh, hell. Now was not the time to be lamenting her lackluster sex life. With a mental shake, Delaney smoothed her hands over the silky gown and walked back down the hall to the studio.

"Where do you want me now?" she asked and noted that Sam's impossibly broad shoulders tensed at the question. He looked up, casually glanced at what she wore, and swallowed.

"In bed."

Delaney frowned. What did— Did he just— She blinked. "I'm sor—"

"On the bed," he hastily corrected. He squeezed his eyes shut and muttered a low curse. "Why don't you lean against the footboard post," he suggested.

"Sure." Bewildered, Delaney walked over, curled her arm around the post and assumed what she hoped was the desired position. He clicked a few shots, so she must have done it correctly.

"Okay. Now on the bed."

Was it just her, or did he seem to be in a hurry? "Uh…okay. Just anywhere?" she asked.

He didn't bother to look up. "Against the pillows."

Delaney propped a few pillows behind her, rested

her head in her palm and bent her legs toward her bottom. The bed was heavenly. He certainly hadn't spared any expense when it came to comfort. She blinked sleepily and smiled. Sam moved forward and clicked off another few rounds of film.

"That's gorgeous," he said softly. "Simply gorgeous. Hold that pose…."

A thrill raced through her. He'd slipped up again and paid her another compliment. Remarkably, she didn't feel self-conscious—she felt…sexy. Delaney turned over onto her back and slowly rolled her head to the side and looked at him through lowered lashes.

Mercy, did he ever look good. Her gaze slowly traced the curve of his strong jaw, the slight cleft in his chin. Those big capable hands manipulated the camera with precision and it wasn't hard to imagine them sliding over her body, doing precisely wonderful things. She bit her bottom lip, her eyes fluttered shut and another warm quiver snaked through her muddled tummy.

"Fantastic… Just a few more." He fired through several more shots, then the telltale whir of the auto-rewind sounded, bringing an end to her session.

Delaney reluctantly sat up and smothered a sigh of regret. She'd just begun to get into it.

"Okay," he said as he did some final tweaking to his camera. "I'll have these ready for you to view in a couple of days, you can tell me which ones you like and we'll go from there." He finally looked up at her and smiled. "How does that sound?"

Like more torture, Delaney decided. She'd done what she'd set out to do. She'd gotten through this shoot without too much anxiety. It was a good step, and for now, it would be enough. Besides, she really didn't want to look at the photos with him. The idea seemed too weird, too personal. "Can't you just mail them to me?"

He blinked, oddly taken aback. "I, uh…sure. If that's what you'd like."

Delaney nodded. "Thanks, I would. You've been great." She gestured toward the dressing room. "I'll just run and change, then I'll give you the address and sitting fee when I come out."

He nodded again, seemingly disturbed about something. "Sure."

Delaney swung her feet off the side of the bed and the whole place went black. "Uh-oh," she chuckled. "Who turned off the lights?"

She heard Sam mutter a curse. "Stay there. The building is under renovation. Somebody must have accidentally cut the power. Let me go check things out. I'll see if I can shed a little light on things."

She heard Sam's bare feet pad from the room, and might have remained there calmly if she hadn't noticed something out of the corner of her eye. A finger of unease tripped down her spine.

Not a single city light shone from the bank of windows that lined Sam's loft. Somewhere between her first and last change of clothes, dusk had fallen and brought night. From this vantage point, she should

have been able to see half of the Memphis night skyline. Not a single pinprick of light disturbed the inky
blackness.

"Sam?" she called tentatively.

"Be there in a sec. I'm getting a flashlight."

Moments later she watched the beam of the flashlight bob into the studio. "Bad news." He winced
apologetically. "Looks like the generator's on the
fritz. We'll have to wait it out."

"Wait it out?"

"Yeah," he sighed. "The elevator won't run without power, and the stairs and fire escape are under
repair. It shouldn't be more than a few minutes before they get things up and running again."

He sounded completely confident that momentarily all would be well, so confident in fact that Delaney didn't think he'd noticed that the entire city of
Memphis seemed to be dark.

"Don't worry," he said, evidently interpreting her
silence for concern. "It's happened a couple of times
since they started the renovation. The guys working
here are top-notch. They'll have things fixed in no
time."

No stairs and no fire escape? She was trapped here
with him for the duration? Oh, hell. She'd never been
good at resisting temptation. That's why she stayed
on a perpetual diet. And Sam Martelli definitely qualified as temptation. "Well, they'd have to be good
if they are going to get the whole city up and running
again."

"What?"

"Look out the windows," Delaney told him, panic making her voice shrill. She gestured wildly. "The whole city is black."

She heard him turn, heard him murmur, "Well, I'll be damned." Then in a more dire, almost desperate tone, "Oh, hell."

"My sentiments exactly," Delaney concurred, slightly annoyed.

"You're trapped here," he said flatly. "In my apartment."

"Yes, I'd figured that out."

He walked over to the windows. "God only knows how long it'll take them to get it up and running again. A major transformer or substation must have gone out. You could be here all night." From the flat, emotionless tone of his voice, a root canal held greater appeal.

"You seemed to have developed a real penchant for stating the obvious," Delaney said, unreasonably perturbed. Honestly, he didn't have to sound so put out. It wasn't her fault that the damned power had gone out. Wasn't her fault that she'd been imprisoned up here with him.

Her sarcasm appeared to chastise him because he muttered another soft oath and abruptly turned and made his way back to the bed. "Sorry," he muttered apologetically and had the grace to sound chagrined. "I'm just thinking out loud. Why don't we go back to the other end of the loft? I'll light some candles and we'll, uh, wait it out.''

Well, it's not like she had a choice, Delaney thought. She slid off the bed and immediately came up against something hard, warm and decidedly male. He shivered—actually shivered—and she could have sworn she heard him grind his teeth. A tense beat passed before he stepped back.

Suddenly another reason dawned for his almost frantic behavior and a slow feminine grin worked its way across her lips.

On second thought, was there any better way to spend a few hours in the dark? Was there a better-looking man to spend them with? *Chocolate-covered sex,* indeed, Delaney thought as the night ahead and all its possibilities loomed tantalizingly before her. Dare she indulge?

4

A DISCONCERTING MIX OF furious despair and carnal hunger dogged Sam's every step as he led Delaney back down the hall toward his living room. She'd slipped a distracting finger through the belt loop at the back of his jeans and followed him wordlessly down the hall. He'd either hurt her feelings by his tactless response to their current predicament, or she'd figured out why he'd acted like such a thoughtless ass at the prospect of her being trapped here for God knows how long with him.

Though he knew she'd gotten more than her fair share of heartache recently—and he particularly hated himself for adding to it—he nonetheless hoped that she'd just lumped him into her men-sucked category and hadn't discerned the true reason behind his blind panic moments ago.

But the thought of being here with her all night, in the dark, with her in that outfit… Sam pulled in a shallow breath.

Damn.

For reasons he didn't care to explore, the idea was almost more than he could bear. More than he could conceivably handle.

Something about the disconcerting feelings this woman evoked scared the living hell out of him, had curiously led him into emotional territory best left uncharted. He didn't like either sensation at all and, though a niggle of doubt had surfaced in his befuddled brain, he absolutely refused to consider the "quickening" as a possible cause.

He'd simply been blindsided by desire in its purest, most veritable form—lust.

He'd taken one look at her and centuries of ingrained civilized male behavior had been stripped away and replaced with nothing but the blind, single-minded drive to procreate. To mate.

With her.

He'd been reduced to little more than a caveman and grimly suspected that if she didn't get out of his loft soon, he'd undoubtedly grunt a couple of uga-uga's, club her over the head and drag her back to his bedroom.

Which would be tantamount to professional ruin.

Which meant she was off-limits.

Sam smothered a frustrated growl. Of all the women in this city, why on earth did his hyper-libido have to zero in on her like a damned homing device? What exactly was it about this woman that had turned him into such a damned lust-ridden, dick-driven wreck?

When she'd gone to make that last costume change, Sam had breathed a tentative sigh of relief. Just the one outfit to go, he'd told himself, then she'd change clothes and leave and he would return to normal. The damned gooseflesh would subside, his scalp would subsist with that infernal perpetual quivering, and the raging erection—which, to his horror, had grown clear out of the waistband of his jeans at one point—would quietly wilt with shame and give him a little peace.

But the sigh of relief had been premature.

When she'd walked back into the studio, Sam's lungs had momentarily forgotten how to properly function. He hadn't been able to draw a breath, much less expel it.

For one insane instant, he'd thought she was naked.

The pale-pink teddy had so closely resembled the color of her skin that from a distance she'd almost appeared nude. And upon closer inspection, she might as well have been.

Though there was absolutely nothing precisely sexy about the plain unadorned teddy, it looked sexy on her because it revealed more skin than anything else she'd worn throughout this shoot. She'd obviously had to work up to that outfit, had saved it for last. The fabric draped the mounds of her puckered breasts, whispered over her curvy hips and brushed the tops of her thighs, revealing legs that were flawlessly toned and surprisingly long for someone so petite.

Sam knew that he'd been abrupt with her, had watched that sweet brow furrow in confusion. But due to the fact that he was rapidly losing both reason and resolve, Sam had known he had to speed things up and get her out of his studio before he did something unquestionably stupid.

Like seduce her.

Now all that frantic work had been for naught and Sam faced the unhappy conclusion that his torment wasn't over, because she'd undoubtedly end up spending the night with him. One could hope that power would be restored to his little section of town first, but he sincerely doubted it. He stifled a dark chuckle. Oh, no. He wouldn't be that lucky.

Instead of wasting his time hoping for a miracle, Sam decided to redirect his thinking and effort where it was needed the most—focusing on restraint. He'd need every ounce of willpower he possessed and then some to keep his hands off her.

Grimly determined to do just that, Sam led her back into the living room where cozy gas logs burned in the fireplace and emitted a little light as well as some much needed heat. He made a mental note to thank his father the next time he saw him for suggesting the gas heat, gas stove and gas hot water heater.

While the electric blower wouldn't kick on, the logs would still generate enough heat to keep them moderately warm. Given the fact his blood had been boiling with need since the moment he first saw her, Sam knew he wasn't in any immediate danger of freezing to death. Still, he'd have hot water for a shower, and the stove would still work, so he'd be able to pull together a quick dinner for his unexpected guest. That was something, anyway.

Sam conjured a smile and gestured toward the couch. "Why don't you sit down and I'll see if I can scare up a few candles?"

Delaney nodded and did as he suggested. "Sure."

Sam padded into the kitchen, riffled through his junk drawer and finally located a pack of emergency candles and a box of matches. He made a quick run through his bedroom and snagged his clock radio from his nightstand before returning to the living room. Thankfully he'd backed it up with batteries for occasions such as these.

He handed the radio to Delaney. "Would you mind scanning the radio for some news while I light these? See what we can find out about this power outage."

"Good idea," Delaney told him.

By the time he'd lit the last candle, she'd located a station and upped the volume.

"...*a jackknifed eighteen-wheeler struck a substation at 5:37 this evening, knocking out power to almost the entire city and turning rush-hour traffic into an extremely dangerous affair. Emergency crews have been dispatched, but officials at Memphis Power are predicting the outage to last at least until the early morning hours, if not longer. Citizens are encouraged to stay at home, as traffic lights are out as well. Stay tuned to WCBX for future*

*updates. All news, all the time. Now let's take a look
at the weather...."*

At least the early morning hours... Resignation
added more weight to the ball of dread rolling around
Sam's belly. He glanced at Delaney and pushed his
lips into a facsimile of a smile. Good news, he'd be
sleeping with her. Bad news, he'd be sleeping with
her. He stared at the top of her head and watched his
career disintegrate. "Well, I guess we need to get
comfortable. Can I get you anything to drink?"

Seemingly distracted by her thoughts, Delaney returned his grin. "No thanks, not at the moment, anyway."

"What about a blanket?" He considered asking
her if she wanted to go change, but for some wholly
self-serving reason, he didn't. The idea hadn't occurred to her yet, and he perversely hoped that it
didn't. If he were suddenly going to turn into a glutton for punishment, he might as well enjoy it.

She nodded. "That would be nice, thanks."

Sam pulled a quilt from the back of the sofa and
handed it to her. Having fulfilled his gracious host
duties for the time being, he sank down onto the
couch as well. He laced his fingers together, laid
them on his belly and expelled a long silent breath.
The firelight cast dancing shadows on the walls and
floors, and the candles pierced the darkness around
the spacious room, lending an even more intimate
feel to the atmosphere. He cast a surreptitious glance

at the woman seated next to him and felt another vicious jab of lust land in his midsection.

Delaney's pale blond hair seemed to glow and move like some living thing as the flickering flames bobbed and climbed in the grate. In the golden glow, in that barely-there gown, she looked like a wood nymph or a fairy, and somehow more beautiful and fragile than ever. His heart tripped an unsteady beat in his chest, gooseflesh skittered along his skin and his scalp prickled annoyingly once more. The perpetual hard-on strained against his zipper, tried to point at her like some sort of damned sexual divining rod.

Sam swallowed a curse and decided to distract himself by tossing an old line into the conversational pond. The silence hadn't necessarily stretched beyond the comfortable—in fact, both of them seemed a little too shocked at the moment to be uncomfortable—but he desperately needed to try and divert his thoughts north of his groin.

He rubbed the back of his neck. "You, uh, mentioned during the shoot that you've done a lot of things lately that were out of character," Sam reminded her. "Besides what you've done here, what other things have you done recently?"

Delaney cocked her head in his direction and a small smile curled her lips. "Well, for starters, I took off work for the rest of the week."

"And that was out of character?"

A soft chuckle burst from her throat. "Most definitely. I haven't had a sick day, much less a vacation, in the last three years.'' Eyes twinkling, she cast him a confiding glance. ''Much to the annoyance of my perfectly capable staff, I have to make sure that everything—*everything*—down to the last little detail is perfect with the catalogue before it goes out.'' She blew out a breath and shoved her hair away from her face. ''I'm manic about it. It has my name on it, it's got to be right.''

Another rumor that held true. He'd heard those things about her and couldn't help but be impressed. It was exactly that attention to detail that had made her business the industry competitor it was today.

''So you took a few days off?'' Sam said casually. ''Sounds like you needed it. Have you got any special plans?''

Her lips slid into a self-deprecating grin and she peeked at him through lowered lashes. ''Other than shipping all the wedding gifts over to Roger for him to deal with when he gets back from *my* honeymoon, no.''

Sam winced. ''Ouch.''

''I know.'' She traced a line of stitches on the quilt with her fingertips. ''Though my staff doesn't believe it, I'm fine. Really,'' she added at his skeptical look. ''Today was simply an off day.'' She shot him a confiding glance. ''I found out about Roger and Wendy and my stolen honeymoon today.'' Her brow folded in consternation. ''Frankly, I was more pissed about the honeymoon. I'd spent months planning that sucker, had seen to every single detail, not to mention that I paid for it. So, in my defense, I really think that I had every right to be upset about that—" her lips formed a secret, almost evil smile "—and I handled it accordingly."

Uh-oh. That was certainly an ominously mysterious statement. "What did you do?"

"Well, like I told you, I cleared my schedule for the rest of the week, and then I drove over to Roger's house and vandalized his yard."

She said it so matter-of-factly, it took a minute for that last sentence to penetrate, and when it did Sam's jaw almost dropped. "Come again?"

She laughed at his admittedly dumbfounded expression. "I vandalized Roger's yard."

"Er, how exactly?"

"Weed killer."

He arched a skeptical brow. "In winter?"

She nodded. "Roger's lawn is green year round. His turf is one of those expensive designer blends. He's very proud of it," she told him. A hard edge colored her tone.

Sam felt his lips tremble with a suppressed smile. "And you killed it?"

"No, not all of it. Just part."

Just part? Sam thought, thoroughly intrigued. He turned to face her more fully. "Okay, I'll bite. What part?"

She sank her teeth into her bottom lip and cast

him a sly glance. "Not much really. Just the part where I wrote 'asshole' in weed killer."

An unexpected laugh exploded from his chest, then tittered out into an impressed chuckle. "Very devious, Ms. Walker. Remind me never to piss you off."

She lifted one shoulder in a small shrug. "I didn't notice you having a lawn."

"There is that," he conceded. "But I am fond of that peace lily over in the corner."

A beat passed, then she said, "I know it was childish, but I just couldn't seem to help myself. And I felt considerably better when I was finished. Almost went back and stole some of his antique roses as well, but I changed my mind."

"Ah...weren't ready to add theft to your rap sheet, eh?"

Smiling, she shook her head. "Nah, not yet, anyway." She expelled a heavy breath. "So what do you think? Think they'll get the power back on sooner than what they're reporting?"

Sam winced regretfully. "I doubt it. If anything, their estimate seems more optimistic than realistic. Still, I suppose it just depends on the damage."

"I imagine an eighteen-wheeler could do a lot of damage," Delaney said grimly. "Wonder if the driver is okay."

"I'd wondered about that as well. They didn't comment one way or the other, did they?"

"No," she sighed. "They didn't."

"Well, we'll just keep listening to the radio. They'll give regular updates. In the meantime, I suppose we should make the best of it. Are you hungry? I could scare up some dinner."

"You can cook?" she asked, surprised. "How?"

Sam shifted and drew a self-important breath. "I use a nifty little gadget. It's called a stove. It's incredible, really," he deadpanned. "It has these things called eyes—but they don't really look like eyes—and they get hot and—"

She chuckled softly and rolled her eyes. "I know what a stove is, thank you. I meant how are going to cook with no electricity."

Chuckling as well, Sam absently scratched his chest and said, "I've got a gas stove."

"Ah," she sighed knowingly. Her eyes twinkled with amusement. "Candles, gas logs, a gas stove. Totally prepared. You're just a regular Boy Scout, aren't you?"

Right down to the box of condoms in his nightstand drawer, Sam thought and immediately regretted it. Condoms made him think about sex and thinking about sex made him think about having sex with her. Within seconds, a vision of himself plunging between her thighs flashed behind his lids, practically burning the image into his retinas.

"I suppose," Sam finally replied and conjured the required smile. "I can make a pretty good omelette. Does that sound okay to you?"

Delaney's stomach issued a hungry growl. She

looked up and her lips tucked into an embarrassed grin. "Does that answer your question?"

"Yeah. Everything-but-the okay with you?"

Her brow wrinkled. "Everything-but-the?"

"In your omelette. Everything-but-the, as in everything but the kitchen sink."

She poked her tongue into her cheek. "Oh, sure. That sounds great. Need any help?" she offered.

"Nah, I've got it," Sam told her, hauling himself up from the couch. He grabbed the flashlight. "Bumbling around my kitchen in the dark might not be safe." On many levels, Sam thought, as another handy vision of the two of them rocking his dinette table across the kitchen floor flitted through his sadistic mind. "You, uh, just sit back and relax. I'll be back in a sex."

Her expression froze.

"In a *sec*," Sam quickly clarified with an embarrassed chuckle. *"A sec."*

Twin spots of humiliation burned his cheeks as he speedily retreated out of the room. A sex? Sam marveled again. Jesus. What the hell was wrong with him? What was it about this female that had knocked him so far off his game? Granted, he'd made a few choice blunders over the years, but today… Sam exhaled mightily. Today he'd simply outdone himself.

Between the physical annoyances, dropping his camera, and now that whopping Freudian slip, he barely recognized himself. This lust-crazed, eternally-aroused, charm-deficient klutz wasn't him. He was a professional, dammit, and charming and smooth. Not today, buddy, a caustic little voice reminded.

Sam grimaced. He laid the flashlight aside, leaned against the counter, speared his hands through his hair and contemplated the probable impact of that blunder. A soft humorless laugh erupted from his throat. Good job, Martelli. So much for keeping things on a professional keel.

If she hadn't realized his problem with her spending the night here before, she most certainly would now. Short of him actually whipping out his rod, he didn't see how he could have made his thoughts any clearer. Hell, only a moron wouldn't come to the right conclusion, and Delaney Walker was no moron. He supposed he could pray for a break in her typically sound intelligence, but imagined that would be an exercise in futility.

He seemed to be honing that particular skill, Sam thought with a derisive snort, because he gloomily suspected trying to resist her would be an exercise in futility as well.

At any rate, he'd inadvertently put the ball in her court and all he could do now was wait and see what she planned to do with it. Given the day she'd had and her sudden fascination and proclivity for acting out of character, Sam didn't know whether to be excited…or terrified. He grunted. Hell, probably both.

BE BACK IN A SEX? Delaney thought as a warm flush of female satisfaction bloomed brightly in her chest.

A slow unrepentant smile rolled around her lips as she watched Sam hastily exit the room.

So her belated assumption hadn't been wishful thinking after all—he *was* hot for her. She bit her lip and her gaze slid to where he'd disappeared a few seconds ago. What a lucky coincidence…because she was unequivocally hot for him as well. A naughty form of anticipation swirled around in her belly, making it quiver with longing.

From the second she'd landed up against his magnificent chest when the power had so fortuitously gone off, Delaney had been wondering whether providence had finally bestowed on her a much-needed break and given her the chance to do the wildest, most out-of-character thing imaginable—*him*.

A thrill raced through her at the thought. She'd always erred on the side of caution, had always done the right thing, and look at where it had gotten her.

Another woman was enjoying the fruits of her labor, reveling in the dream honeymoon Delaney had painstakingly planned.

Another woman was with the man she'd planned to spend the rest of her life with.

That woman wouldn't have to worry about returning wedding gifts—or her china, Delaney railed with a silent, frustrated sob. She'd wanted that china, dammit.

No, that woman wasn't worried about canceling caterers, saving face, or growing old alone. That woman hadn't been weighing the pros and cons of becoming a lesbian. Delaney humphed under her breath. No, apparently that lonely role had been eternally predestined for her. Irritation flattened her lips.

Well, not anymore.

Or at the very least, not tonight.

If she'd learned anything from her new attitude it was that acting on some of her baser impulses was very therapeutic. She'd felt great when she'd pulled that little vengeful prank on Roger, had felt empowered when she said those slightly wicked things to Sam.

Rather than stifling her darker impulses, she'd probably be much happier if she embraced a few of them. Momentarily threw caution to the wind. Frankly, Delaney wasn't sure her nerves would hold up to a complete overthrow of her cautious character, but she was feeling particularly reckless today. And it had been thrilling, so very thrilling just to do whatever made her happy.

Undoubtedly sex with Sam Martelli would make her happy.

His splendidly proportioned body loomed into mental focus and a shivery melting sensation whirled behind her navel and radiated out until Delaney bit her lip in longing. That body combined with the skill and unquestionable talent she instinctively knew he possessed would be a sheer delight for the senses. An adventure of a lifetime.

Delaney blew out a shaky breath as indecision

gnawed at her. She'd never been one to indulge in casual sex, had never had a one-night stand in her life. She'd always been so careful with whom she shared her heart and her body with, and had always considered casual sex as a misnomer. Could an act that intimate be casual? It had never been for her, and frankly, she'd never met a man who had inspired the overwhelming combination of lust and longing that would propel her toward that end.

Until now.

She'd known the moment those masculine feet had come into her line of vision that Sam Martelli was the kind of man who could inspire a cautious woman to be reckless. Her reaction to him had been instantaneous—she'd wanted him. Really wanted him. A wellspring of untapped longing and pure unadulterated primal need had been plumbed, releasing a geyser of sexual energy that had practically washed away any thought of inhibition.

The motivation and the means had practically been handed to her on a silver platter. She was trapped for the night in a romantic loft with the unequivocally best-looking man she'd ever seen on the brink of her new life where men sucked and were ultimately forsaken. At least until she got her head on straight, until she could trust her own judgment.

But who said she had to start right now, this very minute?

After all, would there ever be a better time to indulge in a little out-of-character sensual behavior?

Could she hope for a better partner or better circumstances? In the end, what did she have to lose? Sam Martelli didn't have her heart therefore he couldn't break it. That was liberating in and of itself. She paused, considering, let that semi-profound thought sink in and take root.

Delaney's heart began to race as the weight of her decision gained momentum. A tangled cord of anticipation and desire unreeled through her. She chewed the corner of her bottom lip and her gaze moved to the door where Sam had disappeared. She heard the sizzle of butter hitting a hot pan, could hear him puttering around the kitchen.

In a few minutes, he'd come out of there, they'd eat dinner and then they would have the rest of the night to pass in some sort of activity. Delaney mentally shrugged and a tiny smile curled her lips. It might as well be the one they both wanted and would both enjoy.

Besides, she had the distinct feeling that Sam Martelli would be much better for her self-esteem and general mental health than revenge therapy. Sex therapy with a man who looked cocked, locked and ready to rock would undoubtedly go a long way toward restoring her flagging confidence. Not to mention, just plain fun. What could possibly be better for her than one night in the dark with a man who looked like a sexual god, with no boundaries, no inhibitions—and most importantly—no regrets?

Her lips slipped into another feline grin. Honestly, when she put it that way, it was a no-brainer. She'd been a good girl her entire life. She deserved a little chocolate-covered sex.

5

"WHAT WOULD YOU LIKE to drink?" Sam's disembodied voice called from the kitchen. "I've got water, milk, soda and beer."

"Uh…a beer," Delaney answered. Though beer didn't necessarily go with this particular dish, it wouldn't hurt to have a little alcoholic courage running through her veins.

Sam heaved a dramatic sigh and humor tinted his deep voice. "A woman after my own heart."

Seconds later he made his way back from the kitchen. He carried a couple of Heinekens under his arm and his hands were loaded with steaming plates of huge, fluffy omelettes. He hadn't been kidding when he'd called it an everything-but-the, Delaney noticed as Sam slid her plate onto the coffee table in front of her. Chunks of cheese, ham, mushrooms and bell pepper were spilling out the sides of the dish. It looked and smelled heavenly.

She hummed a low note of approval and smiled her appreciation. "That looks wonderful. Thank you."

Smiling, Sam handed her a beer. "Let me grab a couple of forks and napkins and we'll be set." He headed back to the kitchen and Delaney took the opportunity to covertly study him once more.

Sam Martelli looked every bit as impressive from the back—if not more so—than from the front. Dark brown waves tumbled over his sexy, curiously vulnerable nape, brushed the collar of his shirt. His shoulders were spectacularly broad, the muscles so well defined beneath the flimsy cotton that she could see every ripple, plane, and rise. Could see the slim indentation of his spine at the small of his back.

If that wasn't enough to parch every bit of moisture from her mouth, he also had the hands-down, bar-none best ass she'd ever seen.

Mercy.

It was tight and perfectly proportioned and she instantly imagined it naked with her hands clutched over it. Imagined playfully nipping it with her teeth.

A quiver of longing arrowed through her belly and lodged deep in her womb. Something hot and needy snaked leisurely from one end of her body to the other, making her alternately tight with anticipation and boneless with desire. She wanted him with a desperation that exceeded any sort of rational explanation, wanted him on a level past anything in the realm of her experience.

Sam Martelli was sex on feet and every woman's secret fantasy. He was that oh-so-rare perfect combination of pure masculinity and genuine sensuality. From the carnal curve of his lips, to the languid yet predatory way he moved, everything about him screamed the promise of immeasurable pleasures, screamed unforgettable sex. Hell, even his loft was a feast for the senses. His taste, his very hedonistic nature, seemed to permeate the air. He was undoubtedly a connoisseur of pleasure and Delaney simply couldn't wait for him to share his extensive expertise with her.

"Okay," Sam said as he strolled back into the room. "Forks and napkins, salt and pepper. Can you think of anything else?" he asked.

Delaney shook her head. "No, looks like you've thought of everything."

Sam nodded, seemingly satisfied, and arranged the table to his satisfaction. "In that case, let's dig in."

The first bite confirmed another suspicion. He was one helluva cook. Her lips quirked. Somehow she'd known he would be.

Delaney moaned thickly. "This is fantastic."

Sam washed a bite down with a swig of beer before responding. She watched the muscles in his throat work as he swallowed the drink and felt the bite of desire nibble along her tingling spine.

"Thanks," he told her. "I enjoy cooking. It's a great stress-reliever." His lips kicked into a lopsided grin and a playful gleam danced in his eyes. "As well as being a necessity. It's cook or go hungry. I figured I might as well learn how to do it well."

Delaney imagined he took that philosophy into other areas of his life as well. Suitably impressed, she carved off another chunk of omelette.

"I like to cook, too…so long as whatever I'm fixing comes with microwave instructions." She chuckled under her breath. "Trust me, Martha Stewart I am not. I don't know how to make my own potpourri, or interesting party favors and I don't color coordinate my clothes hangers. I'm a firm believer in the microwave and store-bought piecrusts. I'm hopelessly domestically challenged." Wearing a wry smile, she looked up and her humorous gaze tangled with his. "The only thing that saved me from flunking home economics was sewing."

He arched a brow. "Sewing?"

"Yeah." Delaney paused, wiped the corner of her mouth with her napkin. "It was the weirdest thing. I'd failed at cooking, at household management, budgeting and planning. I broke my egg baby three times before Mrs. Hunter finally decided I was a hopeless case and refused to issue me another one. I—"

"Egg baby?"

Delaney glanced up and caught Sam's puzzled expression. "Yeah. An egg baby. We were assigned eggs to take care of like babies." Delaney poked her tongue in her cheek. "It was supposed to impart the key responsibilities of parenting. Eggs, like babies, were fragile and had to be treated with extreme care. We had to keep our egg baby with us at all times, had schedules we had to follow, feedings and diaper changes, the whole nine yards." She waved her fork airily. "Even had to arrange for an egg-sitter if we wanted to go out."

Sam chuckled and gestured toward her omelette with his fork. "Are you feeling like a cannibal?"

"No." Delaney sighed in mock dejection. "I never managed to keep one long enough to really form an attachment."

Delaney watched him flatten his wonderful lips to keep from laughing. "Because you kept breaking yours?"

She nodded. "Right."

"Okay," Sam said. "I'm with you. Now what about the sewing?"

Finished with her dinner, Delaney leaned forward and slid her plate back onto the coffee table. Pleasantly full, she rested against the couch once more. "I was good at it," she said, remembering with a fond smile. One of the only things she'd ever been good at. "Really good at it. I could look at an outfit, make my own pattern and go from there." She shook her head and smiled. "I loved it, and finally finding something that I was actually good at was very gratifying. I knew from that moment on what I wanted to do. I might have killed a few egg babies," Delaney said with a laugh, "but *Laney's Chifferobe* was born out of that class, and for that, I'll always be grateful. Mrs. Hunter was very encouraging, took extra time with me and really nudged me in the right direction. She was a special teacher."

"I had one of those," Sam replied thoughtfully.

"You did?"

"Yeah." A grin tugged at his lips. "Mine was Mrs. Farris. I was on the yearbook staff my last couple of years in high school. I'd always enjoyed taking pictures, but she was the first person who ever commented on my talent. I'd gotten some really good shots of the cheerleaders and—"

Delaney huffed a derisive breath. "Why am I not surprised?"

Merriment danced in his dark bedroom eyes. He lifted one powerful shoulder in a negligent shrug. "Hey, I'm a guy. What can I say? Anyway, up until that point, I'd always just played around with the camera, had never really considered it more than a hobby. But something about her confidence in my ability sparked a little ambition—" he sighed deeply and smiled "—and the rest is history."

A picture above the mantelpiece snagged her attention. An older Sam and a kind-eyed woman with salt-and-pepper hair gazed fondly at one another. It was a sharp black and white, a private moment caught on film and it seemed to capture the couple's love, the essence of their relationship.

"You're very good," Delaney told him softly, and meant it. Something about the picture tugged at a thread of regret, reminded her of what she'd apparently never have. A family of her own. A couple of big-eyed babies. She longed to upgrade to a minivan, lug a stroller around.

Sam followed her gaze and nodded in thanks. "That's Mom and Dad."

Delaney shifted. "I figured as much. You look a lot like your dad." He had the same dark good looks, the expressive eyes.

"We all do." Sam speared another generous bite of egg. "I've got three brothers, two older and one younger."

"No sisters?"

"Nah." Sam chuckled. "Mom always said that there was too much testosterone in the house."

"I'll say," Delaney agreed. She couldn't fathom that many men and one woman living under one roof. "Ours was just the opposite. I've got a couple of older sisters." She laughed. "Dad routinely pleaded estrogen overdose and headed for the golf course."

"Sounds like a wise man," Sam told her. "Does your family live around here?"

Delaney shook her head. "My sisters are both married to military men. Pam's in Germany and Renea is in Alaska. They each have three kids, are regular soccer moms. Mom and Dad retired and headed farther south. They live in a seniors' community in Pensacola. They're bingo fanatics." For all intents and purposes she was an unofficial orphan. She supposed that's why it was so important to her to have her own family, to build her own nest. She finished her beer and set it aside. "What about yours?"

"My brothers are here, as well as my dad. They

own and operate Martelli Brick, the company my grandfather started right after he emmigrated from Italy.'' He glanced at the picture of his parents and a shadow passed over his face. He drained his bottle. ''Mom died a couple of years ago.''

Delaney's heart drooped with sympathy. ''Oh, I'm so sorry.''

Sam's expression grew curiously guarded. ''Dad's had the hardest time, of course. He always doted on her.''

Delaney's gaze inexplicably moved back to the photograph. That was certainly obvious. She was suddenly at a loss for what to say and Sam moved to fill the awkward silence.

''Let me clear these dishes away and we'll check the radio again for any news.'' He deftly gathered their empty plates and bottles, and strode off to the kitchen again. ''Can I get you another beer?'' he called.

''Sure.'' She felt completely useless letting him do all the work, but what else could she do? She didn't know her way around his kitchen and would undoubtedly bumble into something. Of course, were that something Sam Martelli, then that certainly wouldn't be a bad thing, Delaney thought with another private grin.

Hoping for an update on the power outage, Delaney attempted to turn the volume up on the radio, but accidentally bumped the tuner instead. To her immense horror George Michael's old song ''I Want

Your Sex" instantly throbbed from the small speakers. A short burst of laughter erupted from her throat. She couldn't think of a more fitting song. The hot, blunt lyrics summed up her present feelings perfectly. Sam chose that exact moment to emerge from the kitchen and his step momentarily faltered on the return trip to the couch.

Delaney tucked her hair behind her ear and managed a sheepish grin. "Sorry. I was trying to turn it up." She finally tuned it into the correct station and they both listened attentively as the newscaster reported more information regarding the blackout.

"...*crews still haven't been able to restore power to any area as of yet. Naturally, the areas around hospitals are first in line, but at this time power hasn't been restored to any part of town. Stay tuned to WCBX for future developments....*"

Sam wore a tight, resigned smile and absently rubbed the back of his neck. "Looks like we're in for a long night."

Indeed it did, and there was no time better than the present to make it a little more interesting.

SAM LISTENED TO THE DJ douse his futile hopes about having the power restored one more time and felt himself lose a little more resolve where Delaney Walker was concerned. The spaghetti strap that was supposed to be on her shoulder had slipped down during dinner, and whether she'd noticed this or not, Sam couldn't begin to know.

He only knew that *he* had noticed and his blood had reacted accordingly—it had immediately pooled back into his groin, giving him a whopping hard-on he didn't have a prayer of controlling.

He'd kept his plate in his lap the entire time and had almost sent his omelette flying into the floor when she'd casually licked her lips a few moments ago. His dick had jerked so hard, it was a damned miracle it hadn't burst right out of his jeans.

Despite the sexual torment, conversation had flowed easily between them. For reasons he didn't care to ponder, this disturbed Sam. He wasn't accustomed to enjoying talking to a female he wanted to sleep with. Those conversations tended to begin with a little sexual innuendo and quickly segue into the X-rated, both in dialogue and in action.

Strangely, Sam had been able to simply enjoy talking to Delaney while his thoughts had morphed into a serious porn flick with them cast in the starring roles. It was nothing short of astonishing and, quite frankly, he didn't know what to make of it.

"Are you cold?" Delaney asked, breaking into his turbulent thoughts.

Perplexed, Sam frowned. "No. Are you? I could get you another blanket."

"No, I'm fine. I was talking about you." Smiling, she leaned over and rubbed his arm. "You've got goose bumps."

And now his goose bumps had goose bumps, Sam thought as his entire body reacted from the inside out to her merest touch. He sucked in a slow breath. Shivery heat roiled through his limbs, affected every single cell in his body. The sensation was unlike anything he'd ever experienced. Literally blew him away. Who needed electricity or even a generator? One touch from her generated enough energy to light up the world, or at the very least, his. His scalp was tingling again and the gnashing need he hadn't been able to subdue seemed to have taken on a life of its own.

The word "quickening" buzzed like a pesky fly around his brain, but Sam refused to consider it. This was lust, dammit, plain old-fashioned lust—not some supernatural Martelli phenomenon he didn't even believe in. Damn dramatic Italians.

Annoyed with himself, Sam finally manufactured a forced chuckle. "I'm fine. Just caught a little chill." *That might go away if you'd take your hand off my arm,* Sam thought, though he doubted it.

Delaney finally withdrew her hand, but curiously she seemed to have moved a little closer to him on the couch. One of them had gravitated closer, and given the way he seemed intrinsically drawn to her, he couldn't rule himself out as the culprit.

Delaney shifted closer and raised the quilt. "Here, share my blanket."

Panic seized him. It was inevitable, he knew, and yet he still hesitated. "I can get another—"

"Don't be silly," she said briskly. She spread the blanket over him and settled in against his shoulder.

Her scent and warmth immediately engulfed him. Sam closed his eyes against the onslaught of sensation, prayed for divine intervention. Her naked thigh burned through the thick fabric of his jeans, practically branding him in the process. His mouth managed to say thank you while his mind screamed fool.

"Ah," she sighed, wriggling even closer still. "Much better. Even with goose bumps you're warm."

One usually was when on fire, Sam thought with furious despair. He couldn't think of a single thing to say, so he smiled down at her instead.

And that ended up being a monumental mistake.

The look of raw longing he saw in her bright green eyes combined with the close proximity of her lips was temptation beyond words.

There were a million reasons why he shouldn't act on what was happening between them. She was vulnerable, was an emotional wreck. That in and of itself was more than enough motivation to derail this lust train they both seemed to be riding. But there were other things to consider as well, namely his professional reputation and the fact that he wanted to work for her. Seducing her would undoubtedly wreck his chances of ever going to work at the *Chifferobe*.

Sam knew all of this—*knew it*—and yet he also knew that before night's end, he would have made love to Delaney Walker. For reasons he couldn't begin to fathom, the act seemed predestined, the decision out of his hands.

Delaney's soft green gaze searched his face and she licked her bottom lip. Sam shuddered in response. "Are you by any chance psychic?" she asked in slightly foggy tones.

Sam swallowed, unable to look away. "No. Why?"

Her gaze slid to his lips and lingered for an interminable second, then bumped back up and met his. "Because if you're feeling what I'm feeling, then I want you to read my mind."

Liquid heat slid through his veins at that vague, yet seductively profound statement. He didn't need to possess any telepathic talent to know exactly what she was thinking—his thoughts mirrored hers.

Again, something made him hesitate, made him want to forestall the inevitable. Which was crazy, when he wanted her more than he wanted his next breath, had been forcibly drawn to her from the first moment he'd seen her. He didn't know how or why—logic didn't exist in madness—but for some bizarre reason, he knew that once he took this step— once he was with her—he would never be the same. He would be forever, irrevocably changed…and it scared the living hell out of him.

"Read your mind?" Sam repeated with a forced chuckle, another pathetic bid for time.

"Yeah."

Irresistibly drawn, his gaze slid along the smooth curve of her cheek, down the side of her neck. "Why?"

She stared hungrily at his mouth, bit her bottom lip. "So that you'll do what I want you to do without having to be told." She closed her eyes tightly and frustration momentarily entered her tone. "Because telling you is too hard, makes me responsible, and— And tonight I don't want to be." She opened her eyes once more and her beseeching gaze met his. "Tonight I just...want."

The thin thread of his resolve snapped. "Reading your mind might be a little hard." Sam turned, reached up and ran the pad of his thumb over her mouth, felt another shiver eddy through him. He lowered his voice. "Why don't I start by reading your lips?"

6

FOR ONE AGONIZING SECOND, Delaney thought that she'd read everything wrong, thought the flashes of desire she'd seen tonight were simply a product of her overwrought, wishful imagination. The first tingle of humiliation had begun to sting her cheeks when that careful mask he'd worn throughout dinner finally cracked, giving her a glimpse of the heat he'd banked all evening.

But one didn't dare to play with fire, then expect not to get burned.

It was all Delaney could do not to moan when Sam slid his thumb over her bottom lip. All she could do to stem a sigh of profound relief. The first gentle brush of his lips against hers whipped her insides into a froth of shivery sensation. Her lids fluttered shut under the weighty drug of desire.

With a guttural growl of hunger, Sam turned, framed her face with trembling hands and deepened the kiss. The kiss was slow, deep and thorough—the perfect point between dry and sloppy—and made her blood hot and sluggish in her veins. Her nipples pearled and her sex commenced a steady, deliciously sinful throb.

Sam tunneled his fingers into her hair, angled her head to grant him better access and molded her more firmly against him. He fed and suckled at her mouth, a slow, deep sweep of his tongue against hers, an erotic tug at her bottom lip and then he'd start the mind-numbing process all over again.

Delaney didn't know when she'd ever been more affected by a kiss. Her bones seemed to have melted and any trace of cognitive thinking had all but stopped. Sensation and want had taken over, leaving her with nothing more than the driving need to see this attraction through to the end, to see where this man could lead her.

And, were this kiss any indication, he could undoubtedly lead her to the very zenith of pleasure and back again.

Places she'd never been and would most likely never see again.

With that thought in her foggy mind, Delaney sent her hands on a greedy exploration of Sam. Her thumb skimmed his jaw, rasped against the faintest hint of stubble as she moved her fingers up and into the silky hair above his ears. She pulled her lips from his, trailed her mouth along that chiseled jaw and then down the side of his neck.

Sam shuddered and groaned in response, ran his hand up her sensitive side and then back down again and then shaped one big palm over her rump. Another delicious shiver racked her. She could feel the hard ridge of his arousal against her hip and the idea that she'd caused that uncontrollable reaction in him made her purr with female satisfaction. Her feminine muscles tightened and dewed, readying for him, readying for the evening ahead.

Sam swept her hair aside and nuzzled her neck, causing another tiny shudder to tingle along her spine. His lips tugged at her earlobe, his warm breath setting off another bomb of sensation, and all the while, those big talented hands were all over her, kneading, caressing, and shaping her body. His movements were slow, deliberately sensual and completely unhurried, as though she were a gift to be savored rather than opened hastily. Delaney's lips curled with pleasure.

Perhaps he was a mind reader after all.

Sam kissed her deeply once more, the rhythmic seek and retreat of his tongue a prologue to a more intimate act. He tugged her more closely to him, gently positioned her until Delaney found herself straddled over him, her thighs on either side of his narrow hips, her dampened sex nestled snugly against his arousal. Her thighs quaked beneath the exquisite pressure and a soft, whimpering mewl issued from her throat.

He rocked against her mound, her breath caught and her world stilled and all but fractured.

Sam smiled against her lips and his thumbs skimmed the undersides of her breasts, causing another tornado of longing to funnel through her. Her nipples pouted, begged for his touch. She wanted that talented mouth of his there where his fingers played, and then lower still between her thighs. She wanted an everything-but-the kind of orgasm, the kind she knew beyond a shadow of a doubt that he could give her.

Basically, she just wanted him.

Sam chose that moment to simultaneously rock against her and fully cup her breasts. He rolled her beaded nipples between his fingers, and the shock of the combined sensation ripped a silent oh of satisfaction from her throat.

"God, you're beautiful," he told her, his voice a deep rasp like silk on velvet.

A bud of pleasure bloomed in her chest…then abruptly withered as she realized the implication of the compliment. She stilled.

He could see her.

Delaney buried her head in his neck and swallowed a frustrated wail. Not now, dammit, she thought as the familiar claw of modesty attempted to drag her from this remarkable sensual haze. She squeezed her eyes shut. She didn't want to feel this way, didn't want to second-guess herself, didn't want to be self-conscious. She wasn't that rejected fat child anymore, but a grown woman who'd shed those pounds. She desperately wanted to be with him, to embrace her sexuality, to feel the power of sensation that she'd enjoyed seconds ago. She wanted to be different, wanted this time with him to be different.

Sam scooted to the edge of the couch, abruptly

stood and lifted her up into his powerful arms. "Why don't we continue this in bed?"

Relief permeated every pore and she gratefully relaxed against him. Mind reader or not, Sam Martelli certainly seemed to be able to anticipate her every need, and right now she needed to cloak herself in the cover of night. She couldn't recall when any man had ever considered her needs, much less seemed to put them first. A novel experience, indeed.

An emotion that didn't belong in this one-night adventure momentarily gripped her, but she pushed the tender sentiment aside. She wouldn't allow herself to romanticize this night—he was giving her what she wanted and getting what he wanted in the process. A thoughtful gesture, yes, but no doubt one that was a little self-serving.

Which was fine because she had an agenda of her own as well. "How about that bed in your studio?" Geez, did that sultry purr belong to her?

Sam chuckled softly and quickly changed direction. "As the lady wishes."

Good, Delaney thought as another thrill of anticipation twisted in her belly. She had fantasized about the two of them on that bed only hours ago and now she'd have the cover of darkness and the memory of the set to heighten the experience.

Sam found his way through the darkened loft and unerringly deposited her onto the soft, fluffy bed. He leaned over and planted a leisurely kiss full of secret pleasures and wicked promise. "Hold that thought. I'll be right back."

Somewhat breathless, Delaney nodded and listened to him retrace his steps. She wondered but a second where he could be going before realization dawned—protection. It would have been in his bedroom, not here in the studio. Something about that thought triggered another bloom of delight. If he didn't keep it in here, then one could reasonably assume that this might very well be a first for him. Delaney grinned, unreasonably pleased.

She drew the coverlet back and encountered another pleasant surprise—satin sheets. Another slow smile curled her lips, even as something wicked slithered through her limbs. My, but this man didn't do anything in half measures. Like her, Delaney realized with a curious start. Sam seemed to be every bit as detail oriented as she was.

Seconds later she heard him pad back into the studio, heard him slide something onto the nightstand. The bed shifted as he slid underneath the covers with her. Delaney inhaled sharply as his bare chest landed against her side. He snaked a muscled arm around her middle and pulled her tightly against him. Pure male heat rolled off him in waves. His scent, something earthy and masculine, drifted into her nostrils, curled around her already heightened senses.

His warm breath stirred at her neck. "I believe we were right about—" he nibbled her neck "—here."

A violent shiver shook her. Oy, indeed they were.

And just like that, something naughty and wanton came to life inside her, a heretofore dormant physical sensuality rose above her insecurities, seemingly released by the power of a reckless night with a man that a proverbial wet dream was made of.

Or *for,* as the case may be.

Delaney's palms had been itching to touch him from the first moment she'd seen him, so she slid her hands over his magnificent chest and indulged the impulse. He felt like warm marble, the perfect combination of hard and soft, of powerful muscle and silky skin. All that latent power locked beneath something so innocuously smooth. She raked her nails over his the flat nubs of his nipples, and was rewarded when she heard the breath stutter out of his lungs.

Sam tsked under his breath, rolled her onto her back and slung a heavy thigh over her leg. Apparently, he'd shed more than his shirt, Delaney thought dimly, as his masculine hair abraded her skin.

"It's tit for tat, baby," he murmured huskily. "Just remember that."

Oh, would she ever.

The thought was no more born than abandoned, because at that precise moment Sam's hot mouth latched onto her breast through her teddy and gently suckled. Pleasure rainbowed through her, made her go rigid and boneless all in the same instant. She pushed her fingers into his hair, squeezed her thighs together in an effort to stem the hot rush of sensation.

Her womb clenched and another warm pulse of heat slickened her core. The insistent throb that had begun to beat between her thighs increased its tempo, an unspoken yet unmistakable plea for release.

Suddenly the barely-there teddy made her feel overdressed. She wanted to feel the smooth slide of his skin against hers, wanted every part that made him male against every part that made her female. Her soft to his hard.

Seemingly psychic again, Sam left off her breast and began to gently tug the teddy off with his teeth. Playful nips that drove her mad, made her desperate. He bared first one shoulder, then the next, then continued to gently pull the slinky fabric lower and lower. Delaney felt the material catch on her tightened nipples, felt it give, and then reveled in another altogether more wonderful sensation. Sam's mouth on her clothed breast had been amazing, but that hot, greedy mouth suckling at her naked breast was indescribably perfect. So perfect that it all but brought tears to her eyes.

Her belly grew all warm and muddled, her thighs quivered, and if he didn't touch her soon she'd undoubtedly self-combust. She'd never been so hot, so achingly needy, and she'd never wanted any man more than this one. Something about Sam Martelli simply did it for her. He stimulated her mentally and physically…sexually.

Delaney smoothed her hands over his spectacular shoulders, down his back and traced the fluted line of his spine. All that muscle, that strength and virility was hers for the night. She dragged her nails back up over his ribs, scored them lightly with her fingernails and heard—and felt—a hiss of pleasure puff over her aching nipple.

He licked a hot path to her other breast, swirled his tongue around it several mind-numbing times before flattening the crown against the roof of his mouth. Her breath caught in her throat and her body arched into him, begging for something more.

The tingling trail of his fingers down her trembling belly told her that he was about to deliver more than she could ever possibly handle. Sam drew a couple of lazy figure eights over her ribs and stomach, gradually moving lower and lower until his fingers finally brushed her drenched curls.

"Oh, please," Delaney choked out. Her hips tipped toward his teasing fingers.

"Soon," he promised. "We've got all night."

He was right she knew, but Delaney didn't want to wait all night. She wanted him now, this very instant.

His fingers dipped inside and unerringly stroked her clit.

Then again, Delaney thought as a tidal wave of sensation broke over her, perhaps she could wait a few minutes more. But she wouldn't do it without subjecting him to a little well-meaning torture as well.

Delaney licked her thumb, then reached down and

swirled the wet pad over the engorged head of his penis. He jerked in response, sending his pulsing length into her waiting hand. The fire of lust licked through her veins as she gently worked the slippery skin against her palm.

Sam sucked in a sharp breath. "Damn."

"Tit for tat," she reminded in a teasing, somewhat broken voice. She couldn't have kept her voice steady if she'd tried— Sam had fractionally increased the pressure against her sensitized nub and the intense pleasure was almost more than she could bear.

"Something tells me I may live to regret those words," he said in that deep lazy voice that made her insides melt. He dragged a couple of fingers down her cleft, dipped one long finger inside and expertly stroked a hot button she hadn't known she possessed. Delaney's breath hitched and she pressed against his questing finger.

She parlayed his move with one of her own—she cupped his balls, trailed her fingers over the tight sack and played at the base of his penis until Sam's control snapped and he moved out of reach.

Delaney barely had time to mourn the loss of her toys when Sam spread her thighs, parted her curls and fastened his mouth at her core. The shock of sensation ripped the breath from her lungs and bowed her body off the sheets. He lapped at her clit like a greedy kitten, the rasp of his tongue the most wonderful kind of friction.

"Mmm—" he licked lazily "—you taste good."

Simply imagining that gorgeous head of his positioned between her legs made her insides quiver. Made her feel wicked and brazen and sexy, all of the things she only felt when designing her lingerie. The combined three snaked through her limbs, making her all languid and hot.

The most exquisite sort of tension had begun to build in her womb. Delaney recognized the sharp tug of beginning climax, hungered for it, as she never had before. From the dimmest recesses of her mind, she noticed that something was different about this time, though she couldn't exactly put her finger on it...and at the moment was disinclined to try. Who could think with a hot tongue anchored oh-so-wonderfully between their legs?

Sam continued his sweet assault upon her throbbing nub, then upped the tension building inside her even more by slipping one long finger inside and rhythmically stroking her hot button.

She came hard.

The orgasm pinnacled, burst and sparkled through her, leaving twinkling trails of sensation like the dust from a falling star.

Sam milked every bit of pleasure he could from it, didn't stop his ministrations until the very last quiver contracted her muscles.

When Delaney finally caught her breath and her world tilted back into focus, she flung an arm over her forehead and a sated chuckle bubbled up her throat.

"I've got three words for you," she told him.

Sam settled himself at her side and idly fondled her breast. "You're the best?"

A dark giggle escaped. Oh, was he ever. "Without a doubt...but those weren't the three words I had in mind."

"What were they?"

In one smooth movement, Delaney rolled over and crawled down his body. She took him in hand and made one slow, deliberate lap around the head of his penis. "Tit—" she licked from root to tip "—for—" then took him fully in her mouth and sucked hard "—tat."

His guttural groan drew a smile across her lips.

THERE WAS SOMETHING to be said for a detail-oriented woman, Sam thought, while Delaney tortured him with her tongue.

They were fastidiously thorough.

For instance, she hadn't left a single millimeter of his burning rod untouched. She'd been licking and sucking at him for the past thirty seconds and he already feared that one more tickle from the talented tongue was going to put him over the edge. And that simply wouldn't do.

He wanted to come inside her.

Sheathed in a condom or no, Sam had never allowed himself that luxury. He'd always—*always*—

pulled out. The idea of spilling his seed into a woman had always been entirely too personal. Something too meaningful about leaving his genetic imprint in another human being, particularly a woman he wasn't interested in seeing again. He'd had a couple of serious relationships over the years, but he'd still always felt the same caution, had never been tempted.

But he was with her.

When he'd kissed her...

Sam couldn't even begin to describe the absolute perfection of that moment. Every hair on his body had stood on end and curious whirling sensation had spun behind his navel, seemingly pulling him into a vortex of all that would ever be right with his world. His future, he'd realized with sudden clarity...and then he'd embraced the inevitable—the "quickening"—and now he was going to make her his.

It was as simple and as complicated as that.

Delaney pulled him more deeply into her mouth, curled her tongue around him in the most orgasm-provoking fashion. All that moonbeam hair lay pooled over his thighs, slithered arousingly as she worked him around her hot, talented mouth. He'd never wanted a woman more, never wanted to plant himself between a set of thighs more. The act transcended the physical—he had to have her.

Now.

Sam pulled her up. "Enough."

He heard her tsk under her breath, could imagine that feline grin. She laid down next to him once more, the soft globe of her breast resting against his side. "If you're sure."

"I'm sure."

She stretched languidly. "Do you have something else in mind?"

Sam snagged a condom from the nightstand, tore into the foil pack with his teeth. "As a matter of fact, I do."

"Tell me."

He withdrew the condom and quickly rolled it into place, then moved into position between her spread thighs. His tip nudged at her entrance. Delaney's warm hands moved over his shoulders, down his back and landed on the twin mounds of his ass. She squeezed, making him move toward her.

Sam pulled a breath in through clenched teeth. "I can do better than that—I can show you."

He slowly slid into her, buried himself to the hilt.

Nothing in his life—not even their life-altering first kiss—could have prepared him for the surge of energy that engulfed him. He shuddered violently, every muscle went rigid, and he set his jaw against the onslaught of tingling power flooding through him. It was as though the last tumbler in a lock had clicked into place, simultaneously opening a whole new world to him and forever binding him to her. It was madness and salvation all rolled into one.

Delaney purred low in her throat and rocked those wonderful hips against him, dragging him farther into her heat. Sam gritted his teeth, wanting to prolong and savor the experience and, though he'd never had a problem controlling his impulses, he knew that he didn't have a prayer of exercising any of those tactics with her.

Quite honestly, it was nothing short of a damned miracle that he hadn't come the minute he felt her sweet heat close around him. Still, he'd never been a selfish lover and he didn't plan to start now.

Sam withdrew, then plunged back into her once more, nudged deep. Back and forth, a little harder, a little faster. Long deep thrusts designed to drive them both to the brink. Her body arched to meet his, a perfect rhythm. Soft sighs, greedy moans, and finally the sound he'd been waiting for—a desperate whimper. Music to his ears.

Sam felt the first kindle of her impending release as her muscles clamped greedily around his swollen rod. Delaney slid those small, capable hands down his back and over his ass, felt her clutch him even harder, driving him more deeply into her. She met him thrust for thrust, rocked frantically against him. Thrashed and raced for what they both desperately wanted—release. Her breath came in short, hard puffs, sweet urgent mewls and then a long scream of release issued from her mouth and her entire body went tight with tension.

Her muscles fisted around him, alternately tightened and released and the combined sensations sent Sam flying right over the edge with her. The climax roared through him, brought the edge of darkness folding around him. He came hard, shook violently. He set his jaw against the exquisite, unparalleled pleasure, dug his toes into the mattress and lodged himself firmly—deeply—inside of her while the last shimmers of bright release rippled through him.

He could spend the rest of his life here, Sam realized with no small amount of trepidation. Could spend the rest of his life dallying between her thighs.

When the last tremor faded, he shifted his weight to the side and rolled her with him, careful to keep their bodies joined. For reasons he didn't care to explore, he didn't want to break that special connection. Another first, Sam thought.

A shadow moved from in front of the moon, momentarily illuminating her face. Delaney's eyes were closed in sublime satisfaction, her slightly swollen lips curled into a sated grin. One delectable breast peeked from beneath the sheet, a puff of pink cream nestled on top of a pearly mound. All that silky hair lay spread over her shoulders, spilled over the pillow, like liquid moonbeams.

Sam's chest grew tight with some unnamed emotion and he traced the curve of her delicate cheek with his finger. Still smiling, she turned slowly to look at him through lowered lashes, the gesture one of the most provocative he'd ever seen. She tunneled her fingers through his hair and offered her lips up for another slow, deep kiss, then gently rolled him over, sheathed him again, and straddled him. He hardened inside her, another singularly spectacular sensation.

Delaney leaned down and flicked her tongue over his nipple, lightly bit the small nub, snatching the breath from his lungs. She rocked sinuously on top of him, played at his breast with her mouth and tortured the other one with her hand. He'd never seen anything so erotic in his life, never had any woman so thoroughly seduce him.

"Do you know what this is?" she asked, her voice a husky purr.

She tightened around him, rocked her bottom up and down, creating a delicious draw and drag between their joined bodies. "Wh-what?" Sam managed.

"Tit for tat again, baby. Are you up for it?"

Was he up? If he was any more *up,* he'd explode. Sam chuckled, anchored his hands on her delectable hips and thrust deeply into her. "Oh, I'm up for it, all right."

And they had all night. Somehow Sam knew that would never be enough.

7
_____

STILL WINDED, DELANEY collapsed against Sam's chest and enjoyed the last twinges of another thigh-melting climax. Warm fizzies bubbled through her and an occasional pulse of belated pleasure made her breath hitch in her throat. Her breasts still felt deliciously heavy pressed against his naked chest and, though she'd came so many times that she'd lost count, she knew were he to so much as slide a clever finger over her still-throbbing clit, she'd undoubtedly come again. The perpetually sated smile she'd worn all night brightened even more.

Sam Martelli had the magic touch.

Delaney had listened to that silk-on-velvet rasp all night—honestly, he could make a simple phrase like "pass the salt" sexy with that voice of his—and had done whatever he'd asked her to do.

Without the merest hesitation.

It was as though her body hadn't been hers, but his to manipulate and explore, and by extension, she'd held that same power over him. She'd done things tonight with Sam that she'd never done with another living soul. There wasn't a single inch of her body that he hadn't inspected, a single inch that he hadn't claimed, caressed, or tasted. The tender skin between her toes, the backs of her knees, even her elbows.

Sex with Sam was a full-body experience. He didn't simply hit the high spots and skip to the grand finale. Oh, no. He was painstakingly slow and thorough, seemed to make a game out of drawing out the pleasure. He'd give her just enough to drive her mad—to make her beg—then he'd pull back and start the whole frustratingly wonderful process all over again. He was a true hedonist, a master of seduction, a lover beyond compare. Delaney sighed and settled more comfortably against him.

He'd been perfect.

She'd made a thorough inspection of every gloriously proportioned inch of him. While Sam seemed to take his pleasure by drawing hers out, Delaney had found hers in seeing how quickly she could make him lose it, how quickly she could make him lose that tight-fisted sensual control and morph into the hard, fast, primal lover that bordered just shy of the primitive. He was the perfect combination of tender and wild, of gentle and savage, and he brought out those impulses in her as well—*her* wild side.

Remembered heat burned through her once more. Delaney couldn't explain the unexplainable, didn't know just what exactly had made her shed her inhibitions and reservations, what exactly had made her take the step that she'd taken tonight. Probably the perfect combination of circumstances—the cover of ultimate darkness and a hotter than hot guy.

But she knew beyond a shadow of a doubt that she'd never regret it. This night had been flawless, without a single blemish, and she was suddenly hit with the overwhelming urge to get out and preserve the memory before reality could intrude and screw it up.

Like it always did.

Sam stirred beneath her. "Sounds like you're thinking," he said huskily.

Delaney chuckled softly. "How does thinking sound?"

He drew lazy circles on her shoulder. "It's quiet."

"Funny." She smiled against his chest. "I'd pegged you as a man who could appreciate quiet."

It was his turn to chuckle. The deep, rumbling sound vibrated something inside her chest. "You pegged me right." His fingers inched down and gently brushed the side of her breast, causing the slightest catch in her breathing. "But there is a time and place for everything—including quiet—and this is not it."

Astonishingly, lust kindled again. "Hmm. Is that right? Then what time would it be?"

"Time for this." Without warning, Sam rolled her onto her back and swiftly filled her. Her mouth opened in a silent gasp and her body instantly accommodated, immediately stretched and flexed around him. With a greedy growl, she rocked her hips beneath him, clamped her feminine muscles until she heard the breath hiss through his clenched teeth.

"You p-play dirty," he stammered brokenly.

She coupled the clamp with a hard, provocative arch. "Dirty...works for...me."

Curiously, it never had before, but this seemed to be a night for firsts and Sam and hot, gritty sex just felt right.

Sam withdrew and plunged forcefully into her. "Is that right?"

God, that felt wonderful. Her eyes fluttered shut and all but rolled back in her head. Delaney slid her palms over his chest, bit back a possessive moan and lightly pinched his nipples. She smiled when he shuddered.

"That's right," she told him, emboldened. "Does dirty work for you?"

A strangled laugh bubbled up his throat. "Oh, it works for me. Allow me to give you a little demonstration...."

Sam drove brutally into her, harder and harder, faster and faster. Her tingling breasts jiggled on her chest, absorbing the frantic force of his smooth, steely thrusts. Delaney pulled her legs back and anchored them higher around his waist, simultaneously pulling him deeper into her body and creating an even better friction against her engorged mound. With each furious thrust, his testicles slapped against her aching skin, a singularly intense sensation that caused another steady quake to build inside her.

Helpless, broken sounds slipped past her lips and every nerve ending she possessed screamed with tension. He pushed and pushed, hammered into her until finally—blessedly—the volcano of need he'd forged inside her erupted, sending delicious streams of molten heat through her seemingly boneless limbs.

One, two, three more deep thrusts and, with a roar of satisfaction that made her skin prickle, his back arched in release and he collapsed on top of her. He pressed a lingering kiss to the side of her neck, and rolled onto his side, bringing her with him as he found a comfortable position.

The sound of their labored breathing broke the silence, along with an occasional wail of a siren. The sweet, musky scent of great sex hung in the air. The sheets were a tangled mass at the bottom of the bed, kicked aside and forgotten sometime during the night.

Another first, because even with the darkness, she'd always been too self-conscious, felt too exposed to make love anywhere but under the sheets. Delaney had no idea where her teddy was and amazingly, right at this moment, she didn't care. She'd just had the hands-down bar-none best orgasm she'd ever experienced and she was presently sprawled wickedly naked next to the sex-god that had given it to her...and he was wickedly naked, too. She smiled against his chest. It just didn't get any better than this.

A faint buzz sounded followed by a flood of light as the power suddenly came back on. Otis's ''Try A Little Tenderness'' filled the silence. The light seemed blindingly bright after hours of darkness and, since they'd used this set last, all of the camera lights were positioned around the bed, illuminating them even more.

Her brain seized. Delaney felt trapped in a waking nightmare.

From the dimmest recesses of her mind, she heard Sam grunt, felt him shift beside her. It took Delaney less than a nanosecond to comprehend the gravity of the situation and it took her even less time to become hopelessly, miserably self-conscious and react.

While any other woman might have simply reached down and calmly snagged a sheet, Delaney bolted from Sam's side, snatched the sheet and hurriedly dragged it up over her body. She felt like the proverbial ravished virgin, which was ludicrous given the fact that she'd just enthusiastically committed acts of sexual depravity that would give a seasoned hooker a run for her money. She felt a blush start at the tip of her toes and squirmed miserably as it speedily raced to her hairline.

''Power's back on,'' Sam said casually. If she hadn't been so damned mortified, she might have thought his penchant for stating the obvious less annoying this time, might have even found it a little endearing.

Presently, she didn't.

Delaney squeezed her eyes tightly shut. "Yes, it is." She swallowed. "Would you mind finding my teddy?"

She felt his stare. "Er...sure."

Sam riffled around for interminable minutes under the covers until he finally located the rumpled nightie and handed it to her.

"I'm going to go and make sure that everything is running, make sure none of the breakers tripped when they cut the power back on."

That keen perception again, Delaney noted, eternally thankful. She nodded and accidentally caught his gaze...then wished she hadn't.

Sam pre-sex was incredible. Sam post-sex was simply out of this world.

Despite the fact that she was miserably aware of herself, that her worst fear had been realized—hell, they'd all but had a spotlight thrown on them, for pity's sake. Despite the fact that she was sexually sated, exhausted and satisfied, one look at him negated every bit of that knowledge and the desire she'd felt when she first saw him came rushing back tenfold.

Those heavy-lidded eyes were even more slumberous, more compelling, and his dark brown hair was all mussed and sexy. That in and of itself was enough, but there was more....

He was naked.

And not the least bit self-conscious about it.

Delaney knew beyond a shadow of a doubt that if he'd been dressed in an Armani suit, he couldn't have looked any more confident and at ease. Later, when she wasn't drinking in the very sight of him, she'd envy him that. But right now she didn't, wouldn't allow herself the time. Right now, an exquisite piece of eye candy had landed in her line of vision and Delaney planned to devour it with her gaze. When she'd been mapping his body with her hands, she'd drawn an accurate picture in her mind, but that picture hadn't done the reality of him justice.

Sam Martelli was six and a half feet of perfectly honed male. Her gaze drifted over his impossibly wide shoulders, over his splendidly sculpted chest and taut abs, and then lower still to where twin ropes of muscle bisected his belly and inexplicably drew the eye below his flat navel. Delaney swallowed tightly, and forced herself to look away. Her gaze bounced back up to his and a glimmer of humor danced in dark eyes.

"I'll be back in a minute," he said, then turned and walked casually out of the room. Another correct assumption, Delaney decided as her gaze lingered on the twin muscles of his rear—his ass was perfect as well.

Blinking out a lust-induced stupor, Delaney shrugged into the wrinkled teddy and quickly found a bathroom. Necessary business finished, she paused to look in the mirror. One look at her well-loved reflection made her alternately wince and then smile. She looked a wreck—her hair was mussed, her lips swollen, and her chin bore the definite red of whisker burn. Her makeup had worn off hours ago and—she leaned closer to the mirror—if she wasn't mistaken a small love-bite marred her neck. Her first-ever hickey, Delaney realized with a spurt of surprised delight.

Her smiling lips suddenly flattened. Ugh, she was pathetic. This was what she'd looked like when the lights had flashed back on. While she'd been staring at Sam's perfectly proportioned naked body, he'd been looking at this. Honestly, she looked like she'd been in a fight with a mattress—and lost. The burn of humiliation scalded her cheeks and the woefully familiar rush of self-consciousness made her shoulders droop with defeat.

She'd known this night had been too good to be true, had known if she lingered something horrible would happen to ruin it. The blind panic she'd felt when all of those lights had suddenly come on... Delaney swore, felt a lump form in her throat, and swore again.

Granted, she'd come a long way tonight. She'd broken through a few boundaries and had had the very best sex of her life. But she obviously still had a long way to go before she'd be able to truly conquer her modesty. Baby steps, Delaney told herself. Little victories. The damage had been done, there was nothing more to do now than save face. Clearly a swift but grand exit was in order.

With that thought in mind, Delaney hurriedly found the dressing room, donned her clothes and just as hurriedly repacked her garment bag. She took a couple of seconds to repair her face. After a little powder, a little lipstick and a kiss of chocolate to settle her nerves, she squared her shoulders and returned to the living room to face Sam.

Curiously, she'd never been so nervous in all her life. Her belly quaked and her mouth had gone inexplicably dry. She'd been dubbed one of the most hard-nosed businesswomen of the South, and yet the idea of facing him after all that they'd done to each other tonight instilled a dart of panic right into her racing heart.

Sam turned when he heard her enter the room, and something about that lazy smile that leapt to his lips made her toes curl and her palms itch. He'd taken the time to pull on a pair of lounge pants, but hadn't bothered with a shirt.

"Any breakers tripped?" she asked for want of anything better to say.

"Nah, all was well." He looked her up and down and Delaney got the distinct impression that he'd just mentally removed every stitch of her clothing. "You're dressed, I see."

"Yeah." Delaney tucked her hair behind her ear and gestured toward the elevator. "I, uh, need to get home." She managed to look at him and forced a note of delight into her tone. "Got an early morning."

Something shifted in his too perceptive gaze. "Didn't you take off for the rest of the week?"

Shit. "Er…yeah, but I still have things to do." And he knew precisely what they were because she'd told him. Still, she didn't have to make excuses for leaving. She wanted to go home. Why did she feel so compelled to explain herself? That was something the old doormat Delaney Walker would do, not the new and improved version.

Delaney withdrew a check from her purse and handed it to him. "Mail me the proofs. I'm really looking forward to seeing them."

For a moment, he looked like she'd slapped him, but then the expression vanished so quickly she was inclined to believe she'd imagined it.

"As the lady wishes," he finally said and she thought she detected a slight note of mockery in his tone. He lifted her bag from the floor at her feet. "Come on. I'll walk you down."

"No, that's really not nec—"

"It's late and it's dark. I'll walk you down." His voice was flat and brooked no further argument. So much for a swift but grand exit, Delaney thought, unreasonably stung by his abrupt command.

The trip to the ground floor was tense and excruciatingly long. Mundane conversation to fill the silence didn't feel appropriate, so she kept her mouth shut and prayed for this awkward goodbye to be over as quickly as possible. She peeked a covert glance at his grim profile and then wished that she hadn't. He looked curiously hurt, confused and angry, emotions she recognized all too well. Regret pricked at her heart. Hell, she felt like she'd kicked a puppy. Thankfully, the elevator finally groaned to a halt.

"Well, here we are." Delaney smiled and reached for her bag. Sam blatantly ignored this gesture.

"Which one is your car?"

Delaney frowned and followed him. "The Lincoln. Look, I can make it from here. You're going to catch your death. It's too cold out here." Honestly, he didn't even have on a shirt, much less shoes or socks. Come to think of it, he hadn't had on socks at all this evening. What on earth kept him from freezing?

"I'm fine." Another clipped response.

Delaney pulled the keyless remote from her purse and unlocked the car. Sam hung her bag in the back seat and shut the door, then opened her door for her. Another awkward silence ensued while Delaney tried to figure out what to say. Somehow thank you—while sincere—didn't seem quite appropriate.

"Sam, I—"

His lips fastened hungrily over hers, snatching the air from her lungs and sending whatever thought had been about to come out of her mouth right out of her head. He kissed her hard and deep—possessively—until her knees would scarcely support her and a violent shudder wracked his body, presumably from the cold.

He drew back and that deep brown gaze bored into hers. "I'll call you," he said firmly, and she knew that the promise had nothing to do with her boudoir photos.

Sam nudged her into the car and closed the door. He patted the hood a couple of times, then sauntered back into the building, leaving Delaney there to sort out what had just happened. Five minutes later, she still didn't know but finally started the car and drove home.

OBLIVIOUS TO THE COLD, Sam calmly walked back inside, though he felt anything but calm. His insides had twisted into an angry, desperate knot and for the first time in his life he didn't have a damned clue as to how to proceed. Didn't have a clue what to do next.

He'd known the moment that the lights had abruptly come back on and he'd seen that look of blind panic claim those gorgeous features of hers that she'd bolt. He'd known, that's why he made that cock-and-bull crack about checking breakers, so that he could give her a little privacy.

But he'd underestimated her modesty and apparently overestimated what had happened between them, at least as far as she was concerned, anyway. He'd foolishly hoped that she wouldn't manufacture an excuse to leave, and was unreasonably annoyed—

he wouldn't admit that her rejection hurt—when she didn't stay. It shouldn't matter that she didn't want to linger in his bed...but it did.

It did because she was The One.

Sam knew it as well as he knew his own name. Delaney Walker was the woman for him. He would fall in love with her, she would fall in love with him, they would get married have children and grow old together. The end. This was what Martelli men had been doing for centuries. Why on earth had he thought that he would be any different? How damned arrogant could he be?

Sam had resisted the "quickening," had resisted the entire concept his entire life. Had always thought that the tale was simply that—a tale. But after what had happened tonight with Delaney, he could no longer deny that the Martelli phenomenon existed. His very body had quaked with the power, with the truth. Quite honestly, the idea still scared the hell out of him...but something had happened to him tonight. Something that he couldn't altogether explain. One fear had superceded another.

Sam was still slightly afraid of the power of emotion, of falling in love, but the idea that he might not be able to make her love him in return...now that was just plain terrifying.

He'd experienced the first inkling of that when she'd walked back into the living room, fully dressed and buttoned within an inch of her life. She'd donned her mask, had hid behind face powder and lipstick and when he'd kissed her just a moment ago, he'd tasted the lingering flavor of chocolate. She had every defense armed and at the ready.

And why wouldn't she? She'd just been jilted again, for pity's sake. Hell, she'd been so hurt she'd been toying with the idea of becoming a lesbian. That sensual creature, a lesbian? Sam thought with a derisive snort. He retrieved a bottle of water from the fridge, twisted off the top and took a swig. Smiling, he absently scratched his chest. Quite frankly, after tonight he didn't see how she could continue with that crackbrained plan. He'd made a conscientious effort to pound that notion right out of her gorgeous little head.

Still, with the exception of him—her one-night stand—she'd all but told him that she'd sworn off men, had decided that his entire gender sucked.

Sam grimaced and finished off his water. Given that, he seriously doubted that she would be receptive to the kind of relationship he had in mind.

After all, many men had promised her forever and none of them had delivered. Why would she think that he'd be any different? She wouldn't, Sam knew. She'd offered her heart—her trust—and had it trampled on too many times to think that he would be the one to make it all right. He supposed he could offer up the "quickening" as an excuse, but she'd undoubtedly think he was a nut and swear out a protection order against him.

Sam smiled grimly at the thought, envisioned himself pleading with the police for his freedom when they came to arrest him. *"Honestly, officer, I know it sounds crazy, but she's the one for me—I've got the goose bumps to prove it."*

A dark chuckle rumbled from his chest. This was not going to be easy. But then again, nothing worth having ever was...and Delaney Walker was definitely worth having.

Tomorrow he would seek the counsel of his brothers and father, then launch an all-out assault. He had a lot riding on the outcome, after all.

Like their future children.

8

"IT HAPPENED."

Predictably, the two words momentarily startled Sam's family into silence—forks stalled halfway to open mouths, and every dark head in the room swiveled to stare at him.

Then chaos erupted.

Catcalls, whistles, knowing chortles of joy, and questions flew. The noise vibrated the bric-a-brac stuffed in every nook and cranny in his mother's kitchen.

"Silence!" his father, Gianni, roared from the head of the table. "Mary, mother of Jesus, let the boy speak," he told the rowdy bunch. "He cannot possibly tell us what we wish to know with all this racket." His father gestured to him with his fork. "When?"

Sam swallowed. Somehow telling his family made everything all the more real. Permanent. As if it weren't already? Hell, he hadn't been able to think about anything but her since last night.

"Yesterday afternoon," Sam finally said.

"She came to your studio?" he asked patiently.

"Yes, sir."

"And what happened?"

Sam searched his frazzled brain to try and find the words to explain something unexplainable. When none were forthcoming, he rubbed the back of his neck and said, "I don't know, Pop. I just touched her, and…"

"And every hair on your body stood on end," Mario said quietly.

"And your scalp tingled," Rob added, lost in a memory of his own.

"And you just…knew," Guy concluded.

Sam forced a laugh to lighten the moment. "That about sums it up, yes."

His father nodded gravely, then stood and clamped an old hand on his shoulder. Emotion glittered in his dark eyes and clogged his voice. "Bless Mary, I was beginning to wonder. It seemed to be taking you so long, but clearly that is over now." He smiled and Sam's chest swelled with pride. "Your mother would be so proud."

Of that, Sam had no doubt. His mother had always wanted to make sure that her boys all found the right woman, for them to all be settled with families of their own. Naturally his father's first thoughts were about how his mother would have taken the news. His dad had always been that way, put her thoughts and needs first, did everything in his power to see to her happiness. His brothers all had wives and families of their own—he'd been the only holdout, Sam thought wryly, and clearly that was at an end. But he'd watched them do the exact same thing. Their worlds revolved around their wives and children. It was with no small amount of trepidation that Sam absorbed his fate. He hoped that he could live up to their example, that he'd take to love and marriage the way they all had.

His announcement having lost its momentum, they resumed their meals. His father and brothers all worked for Martelli Brick, the company his grandfather had begun after he'd first immigrated to the U.S., and they would have to return shortly to the plant.

Sam had found another path, and while it might have caused a rift in other families, fortunately it hadn't in his. He handled all the photography for their sales catalogue and various other small jobs, but for the most part, he left the company to them and did his own thing.

His father had been a little disappointed initially, but Sam had always moved to a different beat, so it was no great surprise when he didn't go to work for the company. While his brothers had been playing football and baseball, Sam had been holed up in his darkroom. He enjoyed sports to a degree, but he'd always been more interested in art, in photography, in books. Sam smiled. In short, he'd been like his mother.

Mario, his oldest brother, chased a bite of linguini with a gulp of iced tea. ''So, does our future sister-in-law have a name?''

Sam mentally winced. Now came the tricky part. "Yeah…Delaney Walker."

Guy fumbled his fork, sending his linguini bobbing through the air, and both Mario and Rob made choking noises. His father stilled.

"*The* Delaney Walker?" Guy asked, his eyes bulging.

Sam flattened the twitch from his lips and nodded. "That would be the one, yes."

"The lingerie queen?" Rob clarified. "The one who's always in the paper?"

Again, Sam nodded.

Mario wore a baffled expression. "But didn't she just get dump—"

"The word is jilted," Sam interjected tightly. "And, yes, she did."

Three grave "ohs" sounded and his brothers shared an annoyingly dubious look. Sam chanced a glance at his father, who had resumed his lunch and hadn't said a word throughout this stage of the conversation.

"Pop, any thoughts?" Sam asked.

His father swallowed, cast him an innocent look. "She looks lovely in the paper."

Not exactly the tidbit of wisdom he'd been looking for, Sam thought, but his father was a man of action not words. Still, this was a been there/done that thing for his father and brothers. Surely they could offer some sort of helpful comment. Could give him some sort of perceptive insight.

Sam blew out a breath and looked around the table. "So, now what? Any advice?"

His brothers shared another helpless, blank look that inspired more dread than confidence.

Mario shrugged. "I don't know, bro. You've never had a problem attracting the ladies. Just do what you always do, and remember that this one is for keeps." He pointed his fork at him for emphasis. "You can't afford to screw it up."

"Right," Rob seconded.

Hell, Sam thought, feeling the first stirrings of panic. He knew all that. He wanted them to tell him something that he didn't know. "That's it?" Sam said incredulously. "For years you've been hounding the hell out of me, have been parading women in front of me like cattle on the auction block and *that's* your advice? *Don't screw it up?*"

"What?" Mario's eyes widened innocently. "That's sound advice."

"I wouldn't tell her about the 'quickening,'" Guy chimed in helpfully. "She'll think you're a few bricks short of a load."

Sam gritted his teeth. "I'd already reached that conclusion."

"Ah, hell," Mario said. "She's probably like most women. Treat her nice, be respectful, and *do not lie to her,*" he stressed. His brother grimaced and swirled a wad of noodles around his fork. "Women hate that."

"And a lie of omission is still a lie," Guy added

self-importantly. "I got snarled up in one of those and ended up spending three nights on the damned couch. Not the new couch either, the old one. My back—"

"Only three nights?" Rob scoffed. "Sheesh. Remember that time I told Theresa that I thought her sister was pretty…"

While his brothers compared tortured-husband stories, Sam's thoughts drifted to where they'd been for the last sixteen-plus hours—Delaney.

After she'd left, he'd been too keyed up to sleep, too overwhelmed with what lay in store for his life, and he'd spent the rest of the predawn hours in his darkroom developing her pictures. They'd been absolutely gorgeous, just as he'd known they would be. Some of his best work yet. The idea of working at the *Chifferobe* still held immense appeal, but Sam instinctively knew that was a minefield best avoided. He made a mental note to pull his portfolio from her company. Would do so at the very first opportunity.

The last thing that he needed was for her to find an ulterior motive in his interest, particularly when that motive was false. Sure, he'd wanted to work for her company—was certain that he could have brought a better edge to the layout—but his goal had taken a radical turn last night.

Now he just wanted *her.*

And he didn't have the vaguest notion of even where to start. Sam waited for inspiration to strike and when it didn't, he decided to use a pathetically transparent ploy, one only a desperate man who was choking on pride would do. Her proofs were in his SUV. For lack of a better plan, he could start by delivering them personally.

"Yes, THAT'S RIGHT. Free Elvis memorabilia." Delaney shouldered the phone and pressed her fist to her mouth to smother an evil chortle. Clearly the clerk she'd gotten on the line at the newspaper thought she was crazy, but this was oh-so-much fun. "Yes, in bold print. That's right. And the contact number is 555-4844. Okay. No, *thank you.*" And she meant it.

Delaney ended the call, tossed the phone onto the couch beside her and a let loose a long peal of giddy laughter. She pulled her fist to her chest in a gesture of triumph, then wiped her streaming eyes. Another surprise for dear Roger when he and Wendy returned. She'd placed the bogus ad to coincide with their return and had given his number to boot. Every Elvis fanatic in Memphis—and there were plenty, she thought wickedly—would be calling the happy couple, begging for the "free Elvis memorabilia." Delaney laughed again, pleased with this new vindictive streak. She *liked* revenge therapy.

Despite little or no sleep, this had really been a productive day. After last night, she hadn't been able to rest. She'd kept alternately thinking about Sam and every wonderfully hedonistic thing he'd done to her, to that horrific moment when the power had come back on, and finally, that curiously hurt look he'd worn as he'd walked her downstairs.

If that hadn't been enough, she'd also pondered the meaning behind his emphatic I'll-call-you statement. Somehow Delaney didn't think that it had simply been after-great-sex etiquette. She chewed her bottom lip. Mulled it over for the hundredth time. He'd seemed genuine. But how many other woman had thought that when handed the same line? Delaney wondered skeptically. She snorted. Hell, they'd probably all believed it.

Well, not her. Not anymore.

Besides, to be perfectly honest, she wasn't entirely certain that she wanted him to call her. She'd tried to convince herself that it was simply the circumstances—rebound sex—or whatever, that had made last night so unbelievably special, but she knew better. Nothing in her past experience could hold a candle to what she'd shared with Sam last night. Delaney drew her legs to her chest and rested her chin on her knees.

Something about Sam Martelli and last night had seemed too…big, for lack of a better description. She liked him too much, enjoyed being with him too much. A smile inched across her lips. Enjoyed sex with him too much. Her belly clenched and her skin suddenly felt stretched too tightly across her bones. His naked image swirled into focus and loomed large in her mind, causing a delicate hitch in her breathing. A coil of heat tightened inside her and it took every ounce of willpower she possessed to force the image away.

No doubt about it, everything pertaining to the hunky Italian made her feel *too much*. And at this point in her life, she couldn't deal with *too much*. *Too much* simply wasn't an option.

She'd blindly followed that first heady, hopeful rush of interest and anticipation in each of her failed relationships and she'd ended up humiliated and hurt. And Sam Martelli hadn't inspired a mere rush of anticipation and interest—he'd inspired a flood.

And then some.

Only a truly warped glutton for punishment would want him to call. Delaney paused, poked her tongue in her cheek, then winced when the unbecoming truth surfaced. Guess that made her a truly warped glutton for punishment, she thought with a squeal of helpless frustration. What was wrong with her? She didn't want him to call. She did not. It wasn't called a one-night stand for nothing. It was only supposed to be one night. The end. *Finis*.

Hadn't she decided to work on herself, to get her head on straight and to quit making wrong decisions? Yes, she had and, more importantly, she would. She simply couldn't trust her own judgment when it came to men and, this close to this last catastrophe, she wasn't going to allow herself to be the least bit inclined to try. *Little victories. Baby steps. Men sucked.* Those three succinct sentences aptly and poetically summed up her new attitude.

In addition to the newspaper prank, Delaney had also arranged for another surprise for Roger—River City Bank had lost her account this morning.

She'd never been completely satisfied with the service, but hadn't moved the account because of Roger. Any time she'd try to broach the subject with him, he'd always turned the conversation to something wedding related, the sneaky bastard. Delay tactics, Delaney realized now. He'd always had a hidden agenda, an ulterior motive.

Had this happened before, Delaney would have left the account there to save face, wouldn't have wanted to add any more grist for the gossip mill. Wouldn't have wanted to be accused of moving the account simply out of spite. No doubt Roger was counting on that old mentality, and she'd dearly love to be a fly on the wall when he learned otherwise.

No, this was just a business decision, Delaney thought slyly...with the added perk of being vindictive.

She didn't think that Roger would lose his job over her forfeited account, but he would certainly be called on the carpet. A small comfort, yes, but one she'd take.

There was only one item left on her to-do list today—sending the wedding gifts back. With a dejected sigh, Delaney looked around her living room at the stacks of boxes and a nudge of disappointment landed in her belly. What a waste. All that time and energy spent picking out things to furnish their home with and it had come to this.

Sending it all back again.

To be perfectly honest, she could take or leave the majority of the beautiful things in this room—the Lalique vase, the Waterford stemware, the silver tea service—but surrendering her china again really hurt. Beautiful Wedgwood *Floral Tapestry,* inspired by Josiah Wedgwood's pattern book of botanicals. Gorgeous tones of blue and rose on a background of pale saffron. Both the dinner and salad plates were fully bordered with the heartbreakingly serene pattern and rimmed with twenty-two carat gold. It was a pattern that was similar to her grandmother's china—which, to Delaney's endless frustration—currently resided in her mother's black lacquered china cabinet. She shuddered, remembering. That gorgeous china stuffed in that tacky cabinet was an abomination. Sadly, her mother and sisters had horrible taste.

Having been familiar with Delaney's love of antiques, her grandmother had left her burled walnut dining room suite to Delaney. Delaney'd had the beautifully carved suite completely refurbished and had left it empty, waiting to fill it with her own wedding china. But who was to say that she had to have a wedding to have the damned china? Screw it, she thought, straightening her spine. She'd just buy it and be done with it. Would that all of her hurts could be soothed as easily. Still, she'd undoubtedly get more enjoyment out of that beautiful china than she would have Roger, anyway.

Once the initial pain of rejection had worn off, Delaney had been forced to admit that his calling the wedding off was for the best. She didn't particularly care for his cowardly, last-minute method—which he would pay for—but better sorry now than later, she supposed.

When she'd really sat down and thought about it, she and Roger hadn't really had anything in common. She'd forced interests in things that he enjoyed, manufacturing compatibility when really none was present. Why on earth had she done that? Delaney wondered miserably. What had made her do such a thing? Why did she feel compelled to change herself in order to hang on to men whom she basically forced herself to love? When she'd looked at previous relationships, she'd noticed the same common denominator—she changed to suit them.

Nicky had loved horses—she'd taken riding lessons. Vince had been a football fanatic—she'd learned the game and faked enthusiasm. With Roger, it had been gardening. She had the original black thumb—had killed her air plants, for pity's sake—and yet from the moment he'd shared his interest in the hobby, she'd set out to become a damned expert.

Oh, she was well versed in the subject, could talk about it intelligently, but so far she hadn't been able to keep a single plant alive. The landscaping company came out once a week and took care of her lawn, garden and houseplants. Any deceased plants were quietly taken away and replaced with larger, healthier specimens to simulate growth. Roger had bragged and bragged on her skill. Delaney chuckled. Little did he know…

But why had she done all of that? Was she so afraid of being alone she'd settle for any man, even one who wouldn't make her happy? Was she so afraid of never having a family that she'd marry the first sperm donor she could get to the altar? Or was she simply in love with the idea of being in love? She hated to think that about herself, but at this point she simply didn't know. And until she did, she planned to play her hand close to her vest. No more men until she figured out what *she* wanted in one.

Even Sam Martelli, tempting though he may be.

A thread of regret wrapped around her heart, but Delaney remained firm. The doorbell rang, dragging her mind away from the curiously depressing thought. She'd called a moving company to come and pack up all of the wedding gifts, had given Roger's house key to Beth and asked her to meet the van in Germantown once everything was ready to go.

As a last bit of revenge, she'd instructed Beth to make sure that the boxes were stacked firmly against the front door, blocking the entry. Delaney smiled evilly. He wouldn't be carrying Wendy's slutty ass over the threshold when they got home, by God. At least not the one at the front door.

Still smiling, Delaney swung open her own front door—and froze.

Sam.

"Hi," he said, looking adorably bashful. That lazy grin held just enough uncertainty to melt her suddenly galloping heart. He wore a navy cable knit sweater and well-worn jeans and looked better than good—like capital S-E-X.

"Er…hi," Delaney returned, thoroughly bewildered. Her brow furrowed. "What—"

"You-hoo, Delaney!" Mrs. Carter, her next-door neighbor and personal watchdog, called from her front porch steps. She eyed Sam with snobbish suspicion. "Is that gentleman bothering you? Should I call John?"

Delaney repressed a grin. "No, that won't be necessary, thanks."

Sam gave her a quizzical look. "John?"

"It's her son," Delaney explained. "Occasionally reporters, models and the garden-variety nut drop by. John has been known to physically escort them from my property." Delaney chuckled. "Mrs. Carter is my own personal pit bull in support hose. She guards me well." Delaney paused awkwardly. "What are you doing here?

He pushed a hand through his hair, mussing the curly brown locks. "I, uh, was in the neighborhood and thought I'd drop your proofs by."

"Oh." To her horror, her mind went blank.

Sam's grin faltered and he retreated a step. "But if this is a bad time, I can just—"

Reason returned, along with her manners and a swift diabolical longing. "Oh, no. Now is fine," she assured, stepping back and opening the door wider to welcome him in. "Sorry," she murmured apologetically. "I was expecting the moving company."

"You're moving?" he asked, as he followed her into her foyer.

Delaney's lips curled into a self-deprecating grin. "No—" she gestured toward her cluttered living room where wedding gifts covered almost every available surface "—but all that is."

He arched a brow and whistled low. "Wow. No wonder you hired movers. Where are they moving it to?"

"Roger's."

Admiration tinged his smile. "Ah, that'll be a nice surprise when he returns home from *your* honeymoon."

Delaney grinned and nodded magnanimously. "I thought so."

Sam glanced around her wide entry hall, his gaze lingering on one of her favorite finds, a Spanish Baroque refectory table. "That's a nice piece." He ran a finger over the smooth dark wood. "Black walnut. Mid 1700s, right?"

Delaney nodded, impressed. "Right."

"Where did you find it?"

"An estate sale down in Montgomery."

He drew a deep breath and cast her a conspiratorial smile. "I've been known to haunt the estate sales myself. Antique malls, junk stores." He shrugged one splendidly muscled shoulder. "I've even found a few good items on eBay."

Something warm shifted in her chest and a smile stretched across her lips. The irony of realizing she had something in common with this man—whom she'd just seconds ago mentally swore off—after spending years wasting her time to invent mutual interests with previous losers, wasn't lost on her.

"I've found some good stuff on eBay, too," Delaney told him. "Who knows? We might have even bid against each other on some things."

Sam conceded her point with an uplifted brow. "Anything's possible."

Oh, if only that were true, Delaney thought wistfully. What was it her grandmother used to say? If dreams were horses, then beggars would ride. Delaney blew out a small breath. "So you've brought my proofs?"

Sam started, then nodded. "Yes. Right." He handed them to her. "They turned out great... particularly the ones on the bed."

He uttered the last in a low rasp that struck a chord of longing and conjured images that weren't the least bit boudoir-photo–related. Instead, visions of her and Sam, naked and writhing amid a wad of tangled satin sheets, flipped through her mind like still frames from an old reel-to-reel projector. Desire lit a fire in her loins and her breasts tingled with remembered pleasure.

"Oh, that's nice," Delaney said, in a breathless squeaky voice.

A beat passed, then two. "Aren't you going to look at them?"

Not so long as you're standing there, no, she thought and tried to come up with some reason why she wouldn't want to look at them now, besides the truth.

Which was stupid.

He'd seen her yesterday afternoon. Hell, he'd even told her that she was the most miserably modest woman he'd ever seen. Furthermore, he'd seen her freak when the lights had come back on. He was perfectly aware of her modesty problem and so far, hadn't been anything but tactful and courteous. She didn't have to come up with some bullshit lie. She could simply tell him the truth. Her chest lightened. How utterly refreshing.

Delaney pushed a hand through her hair and her lips slid into a hesitant smile. "Look, the truth is I don't feel comfortable looking at them with you standing right here." She waved her hand airily. "I'm weird about it, I know. But if it's all right, I'll look at them later and get back to you."

Sam's eyes widened in understanding. "Oh, sure. Yeah, that's fine."

Delaney nodded. "Great."

Still smiling, he just stood there and continued to

look at her. One beat slid into five, then he looked away, winced impatiently and muttered, "Dammit, I'm blowing this."

Delaney blinked. "I'm sorry?"

"Nothing. Look, so long as we're telling the truth, I wasn't in the neighborhood and the proofs were just an excuse to see you again."

Delight mixed with that heady rush of interest and anticipation flooded through her once more, making her all jittery inside. "Th-they were?"

The hesitant voice of common sense was trying to tell her this wasn't a good thing—men sucked, right?—but the excited voice of new romance was doing a happy dance, drowning it out.

"I did. I wanted to ask you—" He faltered and another curiously vulnerable smile twisted his lips. "I wanted to ask if you…"

Delaney waited patiently.

"…if you'd like to, uh…"

Any day now, she thought, growing slightly exasperated.

"…go to Martindale with me this weekend?" he finished, in a rush of what appeared suspiciously like sudden inspiration.

Her brow knitted. "Martindale, *North Carolina?*"

He nodded and breathed a palpable sigh of relief. "Yeah. I'm shooting a wedding up there this weekend and…and I'd like you to go with me."

Delaney bit her lip and started to shake her head. "I don't think—"

Sam lessened the distance between them and that dark-as-sin gaze searched hers. He laid a gentle finger against her lips and there was an unmistakable intensity in the deceptively soft gesture. "Don't say no, and don't think. Just come with me."

Delaney sighed. "Sam, I can't—"

He tsked to silence her. His lips formed a tentative smile. "Come with me."

God help her, she was tempted. Still… "Thanks, but—"

His lips lightly brushed hers, an entreaty, a promise. Once, twice, then he sucked lightly at her bottom lip, and when she opened her mouth in a silent *O* of surrender, he deepened the kiss into a fierce, erotic rampage that promised to push her to the very edge of everything wicked and depraved, drown her in redeeming release, and then lead her back again.

Finally, Sam slowly ended the kiss.

Delaney pulled back and blinked drunkenly up at him.

"Please," he told her.

Ah, the magic word. How could she resist a man who knew when to say please? Whom she hadn't met through work and didn't have any hidden agenda? No ulterior motive? One who simply wanted to be with her? Delaney sighed, still intoxicated from that incredible mind-blowing kiss, and then uttered the one word that would most likely lead her down the road to additional heartache.

"Okay."

9

SAM DIDN'T KNOW WHAT on earth had possessed him to ask Delaney to come to Martindale with him. Two days later, with her sleeping form a couple of feet from him in the passenger seat of his Tahoe, he still didn't know.

He'd picked her up just before dawn this morning, and after a few minutes of awkward conversation in which both of them seemed to be wondering just what in the hell they were doing, the weirdness of it all had faded and they'd begun to lapse into comfortable conversation. Delaney had started yawning around Johnson City, and Sam had finally convinced her to take a little nap.

He glanced at her now and something in his chest shifted. She'd dressed for comfort in a soft-green warm-up suit and a pair of broken-in tennis shoes. She'd pulled that sinfully long hair over one shoulder and plaited it into one long, thick braid that slid enticingly over her breast every time she moved. Sam's fingers had been itching to loosen that braid all morning, itching to divide those long strands one section at a time until it all hung loose around her shoulders again.

Delaney'd had a little over a day to call and cancel on him, and Sam had waited grimly for that call. He'd fully expected her to bail, and he hadn't breathed a sigh of relief until this morning when he'd knocked on her door and found her dressed, with her bags sitting at her feet.

When he'd gone over to her house Wednesday afternoon, he hadn't planned to ask her to go to Martindale with him. He'd had no plan whatsoever. He'd just needed to see her again, to make sure that everything hadn't been a fluke. He'd known it hadn't, of course, but he'd still needed to see if he felt the same buzzing sensation when he saw her again.

He had.

And the condition had only worsened.

More goose bumps, more tingling scalp, more desire and, astonishingly, more need. He'd taken one look at her and gone instantly hard. He could have taken her on the refectory table, or against the front door. Wherever. He'd just wanted her. Sam made a mental note to ask his brothers about this. Hell, if this sensation only intensified as their relationship progressed, he didn't know if he'd survive the damned "quickening."

The combination of anxiety and attraction had all but rendered him mute. His brothers' don't-screw-it-up advice had been ringing in his ears, his scalp had been prickling annoyingly, and his rod had almost swelled out of jeans. Then she'd smiled that awkward *time-to-get-out-of-my-house* smile—Sam knew that smile—he'd worn it several times—but had never had it directed at him. And he'd panicked. He'd known that he had to come up with something and the only thing that had popped into his near-paralyzed brain was Martindale.

But the more he'd thought about it, the better he liked the idea. He was shooting this particular wedding at Grand Court on Ravenwood Estate, a brand new four-star hotel situated on the pastoral grounds of the Estate, a two-hundred and seventy-five room French Renaissance-style palace nestled in the Blue Ridge mountains. The house was cram-packed full of original furnishing and art objects collected by the late owner, Remington Rutledge. It was awe-inspiring, particularly to history buffs and antique lovers. Delaney, he knew, would love it. She'd confessed that she'd never been to the estate, but that she'd always wanted to go. Her eyes had taken on a particularly keen sparkle while they'd talked about it.

In addition to the house, the grounds in and of themselves were a sight to behold. The gardens were spectacular, and the estate boasted a winery as well. Were that not enough, little antique stores littered the downtown area, a veritable Garden of Eden to an old-stuff junkie.

For a weekend getaway, Sam knew he couldn't have picked a better place. He'd be working off and on throughout the weekend, but there would be plenty of time for them to get out and explore during the day, and other than the after-rehearsal dinner, they'd have the nights to themselves as well.

Sam didn't want to push Delaney—he instinctively knew that tactic wouldn't work with her, particularly right now. But he also knew that time was of the essence. They'd shared a phenomenal night together and she'd either been so unmoved or spooked by it that she'd left, rather than spend the night with him. Sam preferred to think that she'd been spooked. Given the night they had, the alternative simply wasn't possible.

To further give him pause, when he'd made that unexpected visit to her house, she'd been ready to show him the door only minutes after he'd arrived. Sam knew she wasn't interested in anything permanent with him. Intrigued by him? Yes. Attracted to him? He mentally snorted. No doubt.

But she'd made it perfectly clear that she was no longer interested in any long-term relationship. She was keeping him at arm's length. He could feel it. Though she'd been perfectly amiable, she'd been guarded as well. She'd been just flirtatious enough to let him know what she wanted out of this weekend—sex. She wanted a weekend with no worries, no strings, and no emotional involvement. She wanted to indulge in a little scandalous behavior— the kind she'd been accused of, but had clearly never participated in—wanted to test her limits and stretch her boundaries. In short, she wanted his body, which under normal circumstances would have been equally agreeable and flattering.

But these were hardly normal circumstances.

Sam didn't just want her for the weekend—he wanted her forever.

His wolflike genes had howled at her, singled her out as The One. As bizarre as it sounded, he *knew* it, and knowing it made it all the more nerve-racking. He couldn't afford to screw things up with her, couldn't put a single toe out of line—to that end, he'd called and formally withdrawn his portfolio from her company. That was a potential bomb he didn't want blowing up in his face and he instinctively knew it had the potential to be catastrophic. He didn't know why, but the warning was there all the same.

Nevertheless, he still didn't know quite how to proceed. He'd been denying the Martelli phenomenon since puberty, had decided when his mother died that marriage simply wasn't for him. He'd honed his seduction skills, but had never—*never*—once considered how one might go about attracting a female permanently. He'd never had the need.

Until now.

Sam blew out a silent breath and his gaze inexplicably darted to the woman in his passenger seat. Need and something else, something desperate, landed a blow to his midsection, making his fingers tense on the steering wheel.

Oh, hell, Sam thought. Hopefully, those wolflike

genes that had pointed her out as The One would also lead him in the right direction when it came to making her his. God knows he was going to need all the help he could get, because frankly, while he knew exactly what buttons to push to make her come, he didn't have any idea how to go about making her happy…or making her his.

DELANEY DIDN'T KNOW how much longer she could feign sleep. She'd been awake for the last several miles, though she hadn't betrayed so much as a blink or a muscle twitch. Sam had plugged CCR into the CD player and "Proud Mary" currently played on his customized system.

Though his tastes clearly leaned to the old and eclectic, he nonetheless had a savvy sense of current technology. She'd noticed a sophisticated computer system in his loft, as well as a top-of-the-line plasma TV. Both were pricey items and she'd concluded that his business had to be extremely lucrative to support his discriminating tastes.

For that matter, his antiques hadn't come cheap either. She'd noticed—and coveted—a Victorian Davenport desk, among other things, that would have required a substantial amount of cash to own.

Delaney had been trying since Wednesday afternoon to figure out what exactly had made her agree to come on this trip, and then wondered even more what had possessed her not to call and cancel it.

Now, easily three hundred miles from home, she still hadn't figured it out.

She'd alternately berated herself, and then wondered what to pack. How screwed up was that? Still, Sam had unwittingly hit upon a hidden desire and a weakness—she'd wanted to see the Ravenwood Estate for years, but had never had the time—nor made it—to make the trip. She'd always been too busy at work, or learning some other new hobby to make someone else happy. Never enough time for herself.

If he had asked to go anywhere but there, she most likely would have said no. Common sense, she hoped, would have prevailed. But the combined temptation of the trip and a weekend spent in his bed—on top of, beneath, and next to his wonderful body—was simply more than she could pass up. Given the chance, Sam Martelli could become every bit as addictive to her as chocolate.

It would have been extremely difficult just to pass up the weekend in his bed part—Delaney inwardly shuddered with a blast of desire—but given the wary intensity of her feelings, she was almost certain that she would have told him no.

In fact, though she'd been absolutely melting inside, she'd been ready to show him the door seconds after she'd opened it and found him standing on her front porch. She'd firmed her resolve, had been mentally chanting her new men-sucked, baby-steps, little-victories cheer.

But one thought-shattering brush of his sexy lips

against hers, one tender entreaty, and a promised trip to a place she'd always wanted to go...and every bit of that resolve had been blown away like a dandelion seed in a soft wind.

If he'd taken her lips in a kiss designed to conquer, in one that had made her a slave to the attraction, Delaney knew she would have declined the invitation. She would have been irritated enough to have said no. But apparently—frighteningly—Sam had known that as well, and had done the one thing guaranteed to make her capitulate—he'd persuaded, not pressed.

The fact that he'd seemed genuinely interested in spending time with her—*just her*—and didn't want to further his own career via her success was no small part of her decision as well. Unlike losers one and two, he wasn't shopping for a job, shopping for an account. It was heartily refreshing.

Rather than continuing to chastise and berate herself for being a fool, Delaney had decided to take advantage of what he'd offered. His invitation couldn't have come at a better time. She'd taken off the rest of the week, so her schedule was clear and, despite that one embarrassing moment when the light had blown her cover of darkness at Sam's, she'd still made a tremendous amount of progress when it came to her modesty.

Besides the incredible night spent with Sam, one look at her pictures had told her that.

After Sam had left, Delaney had held her breath

and cautiously opened her packet of boudoir photos. She'd barely recognized the woman in those pictures as herself. To say that she'd been surprised would have been a vast understatement—she'd been completely shocked.

The first few shots, she'd been tense and had worn a hesitant smile but still looked surprisingly...sexy. Looking at them with a critical eye, she could honestly say that she looked good. Not great. She'd never be cover-model material. Delaney inwardly chuckled. Even if she could forego a little thing like food, she'd been genetically built on a small, hippy scale. But she was healthy and toned, and she supposed something could be said for that.

As the session had progressed, she'd relaxed and Delaney could see first the spark of lust, then the steady build of fire, as frame by frame, her lips curled just a little more seductively, her body grew just a little more languid. A wicked gleam had danced in her eyes and she'd looked happy, for lack of a better description. Sam had done a fantastic job of capturing *her* on film. More than her body, and her designs, just her.

Delaney had critically studied the pictures, sized them up professionally, and had come to the conclusion that Sam Martelli had one incredible eye, unparalleled talent. Lighting, composition, positioning, every detail was perfect. Were he not so obviously successful, she'd be inclined to offer him a position at the *Chifferobe*. Still might, for that matter. Sam's photography was edgy and compelling, very sensual.

While her current staff of photographers did an admirable job, there was always room for improvement and his talent could definitely improve her catalogue. It was something to think about, anyway.

Delaney felt her body shift as he smoothly pulled the SUV off what she could only assume was an exit ramp. She didn't think they'd had time to make it to Martindale yet, but who knew how long she'd been asleep? It could have been thirty minutes or three hours. Still, she hadn't gotten a great deal of rest over the past few days, and her mouth had that dry, stale taste that indicated she'd been out for a while, anyway. She could use a bathroom break and something to drink.

She stretched, blinked sleepily and pretended to wake up. Sam looked over at her and smiled, making her heart skip a beat. "Hey," he murmured. "Get enough rest?"

He wheeled the SUV into a gas station and pulled up next to a pump. Delaney shifted gingerly. "Yeah, I did." She stifled a genuine yawn. She looked around, trying to see any distinguishing landmarks. "Where are we?"

Sam shifted into park and killed the ignition. "Almost there. We're about thirty miles outside of Martindale. I'm going to fill up and grab a snack and a drink." He arched a brow. "Can I get you anything?"

"Nah, I'll get it." She offered him a small smile. "I've got to find the little girls' room, anyway."

Sam nodded, and moved to take up the pump. Delaney strolled into the store, found the bathroom and attended to necessary business. When she came out, Sam had already grabbed a soda and was trolling the candy aisle.

The sheer perfection of him, the sheer size, hit her once more and something hot and achy vibrated in her belly. He towered over everyone else, dominated the space around him. Those dark brown locks were windblown, messy almost, and lent a curiously boyish look to his ruggedly handsome Italian features. His lean cheeks were slightly red from the cold. He wore a long-sleeved brushed flannel shirt in shades of green and gray tucked into a pair of worn, comfortable-looking button-fly jeans that hugged his muscular thighs and molded over that fist-bitingly wonderful ass.

A fire ignited in her womb, blazed up through her belly and licked her nipples. The breath stuttered out of her lungs in a small whoosh of longing and every wickedly depraved wonderful thing he'd done to her the night before last immediately leapt to mind. He looked up, smiled and absently licked his lips.

Astonishingly, Delaney imagined that talented tongue of his licking her in the most intimate of places. Remembered what he'd felt like there, between her legs, feasting on her until her body had bowed off the sheet and she'd screamed her release into the night.

She was standing in the middle of a convenience store in God knows where, holding a chocolate Yoo-Hoo and *this* was what she was thinking. It was crazy. Insane. She was hit with the almost insatiable urge to drag him into the bathroom, turn off the light and have him take her hard and fast against the damned door, the way she'd never been taken. Her sex slickened, drenching her panties.

Something about what she'd been thinking must have shown on her face, because a blatantly sexy oh-so-knowing gaze glimmered in those overtly hungry dark eyes and he carelessly put down his selections and stalked purposefully toward her. Delaney held his gaze, bit her bottom lip as a thrill raced through her, reckless and willing.

"Come on," Sam said roughly. He threaded her fingers through his and determinedly tugged her back toward the bathroom. Anticipation sang in her blood, forcing a stuttered laugh from her throat. She thought she heard herself say okay, but couldn't be sure.

Sam opened the door for her, then followed her inside. He simultaneously backed her against the door and flipped the lock, then framed her face with his hands and his mouth came down hungrily on hers. The first taste of him exploded on her tongue, made a low purr of approval sound in the back of her throat. He answered her purr with a greedy growl, sucked at her tongue, fed at her mouth.

Delaney wound her arms around his neck and pressed herself against him, shamelessly begging for whatever he could give her. Her body craved his, desperately needed an orgasmic fix. Her pulse beat hotly between her legs, making her squirm more closely to him. Her nipples were pearled, her breasts achingly heavy and need raked across every nerve ending.

She felt him hard against her belly and groaned into his mouth. God, how she wanted him. She couldn't get close enough to him, though she'd practically scaled his body and crawled under his skin.

Sam left off her mouth and trailed a hot brand of sensation down her neck, and then lower still into the valley between her breasts. He reached and tweaked a nipple, forcing a startled "oh" from her lips. He bent down, sucked her through the thin fabric and wrenched another sound of pleasure from her throat. He positioned his hips between her legs and rocked in that absolute perfect place, one of the brass buttons from his jeans hitting squarely on her throbbing clit. Delaney's mouth opened in a silent gasp, and she pressed herself even harder against him, frantically mimicked his thrusting hips in a perfect rhythm. The bright sparkle of release hovered just out of reach and she so desperately wanted it.

Needed it.

Breathing hard, Sam left off her breast and increased the pressure and tempo beneath her waist. "Tell me what you want."

Oh, God.

Delaney whimpered softly. She wanted him, dammit. "You know," Delaney said brokenly, her voice a pleading rasp. And he did. He just wanted to make her say it, wanted to hold her accountable this time.

Sam's mouth found hers once more, suckled and fed, a hot thrilling mating of the tongues that simulated the exact thing that she wanted.

"Say it," he told her, his voice husky with want.

Delaney squeezed her eyes shut. She was mindless with need, was practically coming out of her burning skin. Her breathing came fast and sharp and every cell in her body clamored for him to fill her, for him to push her to the edge of ecstasy and back again. She felt hollow and empty and needed him inside her more than she needed her next breath. It was madness. Insane. Wonderful.

"You," she gasped. "I need *you.*"

Sam smiled against her lips, then blindly reached over and flipped the light switch into the off position, sending the small room into immediate darkness. For her, she knew. The thoughtful gesture made her chest tight, and when she could think clearly again, she'd properly thank him for it. But right now—

Sam reached down and pushed her pants and undies down and off, then dragged a couple of talented fingers through her drenched curls, fragmenting her thoughts.

"God, you're wet."

Delaney cupped him through his jeans. "You're hard."

He strangled on a laugh. "Well, that happens when you look at me...."

Delaney made swift work of the button closures, worked his pants and boxers down and wrapped her hand around the long, hard length of him. "Look at you like what?" Delaney asked distractedly.

Sam pushed himself against her hand once, then growled, drew back and fished a condom from his pocket and swiftly rolled it into place. "Like... nothing. I get hard when you look at me." He chuckled. "Have been hard since I met you."

Warm delight bloomed in her chest. "Well, I guess we're even then. I've been wet since I met you."

"Good," he said thickly. "That means we'll always be ready."

"Ready for what?"

"This." Sam lifted her off the floor, forcing her to anchor her legs around his waist, then leaned her back against the door and slid into her in one long, swift movement that was instantly satisfying, yet somehow insufficient. Delaney let out a small gasp, clenched her aching muscles around him and wrapped her arms more tightly around his neck.

Sam found her mouth in another searing kiss and pumped frantically in and out of her, harder and faster, then harder still. Her belly quickened, her thighs tensed and she hovered on the brink of release.

Seemingly sensing her nearness, Sam abruptly changed tempo, still fantastic, but not enough to give her what she wanted.

The greedy sadistic wretch.

"Sam," she pleaded, the frustration sweet. She clamped her muscles around him, equally dreading and enjoying the hot seek and retreat of his body inside hers.

Sam sucked in a tight breath and squeezed her bottom. "Say please," he told her, a trace of laughter in his tone, clearly enjoying the power she'd unwittingly given him.

Oh, no, Delaney thought. She'd already begged him once. She wouldn't do it again. She used her vulnerable position as best she could and arched up and away from him, limiting his access into her body.

Sam tried to push farther into her, but he'd failed to remove his pants and his effort was hampered. She, on the other hand, while braced against the door, could use his shoulders to lift herself up and away from his questing thrusts. He was still inside her, but not as deeply, and clearly, Delaney thought when she heard his dark chuckle, not as far as he wanted to be.

"Oh, y-you are evil," he stuttered breathlessly, and this time a hint of admiration was there.

He tried once more to bring her hips down, but Delaney remained firm, pushed herself against his shoulders. This time, he was the one who half groaned, half laughed in frustration. "Delaney," he growled brokenly, desperately trying to lodge himself more deeply inside her.

A thrill of feminine power raced through her. She kept herself annoyingly out of his desired reach. "Yes?"

"Please," he finally relented.

Delaney sagged and he plunged fully into her. He pumped hard and fast, thrillingly pistoned in and out of her until she felt the tight screw of release finally snap and the sparkling burn of sensation burst and rain through her. He caught her scream of release in his mouth, ate every long orgasmic syllable of it as her body spasmed around his.

Three, four, five furious thrusts later, her legs still quaking, Sam's big body tensed and she felt a pool of heat press against her womb, giving her another deep sparkler of pleasure.

An abrupt knock at the door startled both of them. "Is everything all right in there?" a man's voice called.

Delaney buried her head in his shoulder to keep from laughing, and she felt a chuckle vibrate Sam's chest.

"Er…yes," Sam said brokenly. "Everything's fine." Delaney detected a slight note of innuendo in his voice and had to smother another laugh.

"Okay," the voice returned, somewhat hesitantly. "Just wanted to make sure."

"We're fine," Sam repeated.

"Sir, are you aware that you're in the women's rest room?"

Delaney couldn't help it. She couldn't suppress a chuckle.

Sam's forehead touched her shoulder. "I am now," he told him.

"Ma'am, are *you* all right in there? Do I need to call anyone?"

Oh, Lord. The attendant obviously thought she'd been dragged into the bathroom against her will. Sam tensed, then she felt another laugh shake his shoulders as realization dawned.

"I'm fine," Delaney called. "No need to call anyone. Everything is fine."

"Okay," he called hesitantly, and they heard him shuffle away.

They both dissolved into quiet laughter, then quickly dressed and hurried from the bathroom. Delaney double-timed it back out to the SUV and when Sam joined her, he was distinctly red-faced and wore an adorably grim smile.

"I'm so glad I don't ever have to see that man again," he said fervently. He exhaled mightily and slid his soda into the cup holder, then tossed her the candy bar she'd asked for. "The way he acted, you'd think he was your father. Started lecturing me about premarital sex and social diseases." He shuddered.

Delaney frowned. "Sam?"

He cast her a glance. "Yeah?"

"Where's my Yoo-Hoo?"

His expression turned comically pained. "Ah, hell," he said, then opened the door and retraced his steps back into the store.

Delaney laughed. She might have been unforgivably stupid for accepting this invitation...but being stupid with Sam was a lot more fun that being smart alone.

At least, for the moment, anyway.

10

THE LONG WINDING DRIVE over the rolling hills and gentle valleys, and over the occasional stone bridge toward the estate was absolutely gorgeous, but her first glimpse of the mansion pushed a reverent ooh of wonder from her mouth and made her lean slightly forward in her seat.

Pictures, while accurate, didn't do justice to the sheer beauty, the mammoth size, of the gorgeous limestone castle. The stonework, the incredible attention to detail was visible even from this distance.

Sam smiled over at her, clearly pleased with her awed enthusiasm. "It's amazing, isn't it?"

"Yes," she breathed, unable to drag her mesmerized gaze away. "So you've been here before?"

He nodded. "Many times. I try to make the trip at least a couple of times a year. It's breathtaking in the fall when the leaves change in the mountains. I like to canoe down the river behind the estate and just take it all in. I've gotten several really good shots. Have even sold a few." He lifted one powerful shoulder in a negligent shrug. "And at Christmas, it's absolutely spectacular. Over fifty trees throughout the mansion and every room is decorated to the nines.''

"It sounds fantastic," Delaney said.

"It is. Then in the spring, when the gardens are in full bloom…" He cast her one of those sexy-as-sin smiles. "Now, that is something to see. The Walled Garden has something like fifty thousand bulbs, tulips, daffodils, and Dutch iris. It's supposed to be one of the best examples of an English garden here in the States."

Delaney nodded absently and continued to stare at the house as they drew closer and closer. A huge oblong fountain sat in the middle of a large, perfectly manicured courtyard. In turn, the courtyard was surrounded by a tree-lined cobblestoned drive that stretched out before the house and highlighted the massive size of the house. Excitement bubbled through her, pushing her lips into an irrepressible smile.

"In the summer they hold concerts out on the North Terrace. I came up one year and saw Billy Joel."

"Really?"

"Yeah. It was great." He pulled through the wrought iron gates that led to the Grand Court. "There's always something going on up here and it doesn't get any more beautiful. I really think that you'll enjoy it."

"Oh, I know I will." She had no doubt and she couldn't wait to get up to the house and start exploring. Delaney's spirits drooped when a thought occurred to her. "Do you have to get immediately to work as soon as we get here?"

"Nah, not immediately," Sam said, to her vast relief. "I thought we could check in, grab a bite to eat and go ahead and tour the house today. There are a couple of other tours we can take tomorrow—the rooftop tour and a behind-the-scenes tour that's really worth seeing—then there's the winery and the gardens and there are a couple of antique shops downtown that I'd like to hit before we leave. Does that sound all right with you?"

"Sure," she told him. In fact, she couldn't have planned a more perfect weekend if she'd arranged it herself, Delaney thought, equally delighted and dismayed. Honestly, it was downright eerie how he seemed to be able to do just the right thing, say the right thing and always do it at exactly the right moment. Her muscles clenched with remembered pleasure and a flush warmed her from the inside out.

Like the bathroom.

She'd looked at him and thought about making it against the bathroom door—she, who had never had sex anywhere but in a good old-fashioned bed—and he'd stalked across that store, looked at her like she assumed the Big Bad Wolf would have gazed at Little Red Riding Hood, then hauled her into the bathroom and had proceeded to do precisely what she'd wanted him to do—take her hard and fast against the door.

It was almost as if he had a direct line into her thoughts, some mystical connection. Delaney dismissed the fanciful thought as ludicrous. He couldn't know her thoughts. He was just extremely perceptive and shared some of her interests. That was the novelty, Delaney decided. She'd never met a man like Sam Martelli.

Her gaze slid to him, lingered puzzlingly on his handsome profile while she tried to find some category he would fit into, but she'd just as well try to fit a square peg into a round hole. Sam was a niche onto himself. Defied categorizing. Like her, an annoying little voice whispered in her ear.

Just then the Tahoe crested a small hill and the Grand Court immediately loomed into view, forcing her thoughts away from that curiously revealing line of thinking. Pale gray in color, the grand exterior closely resembled the look of the mansion. Lots of windows and turrets, and spectacularly landscaped. Very posh.

Sam pulled up under the porte cochere. He handed the key to the valet, while another attendant opened her door. Within seconds their luggage and his equipment had been smoothly removed from the SUV and wheeled into the lavish hotel lobby. Soaring ceilings, maple-paneled walls and dark cream marbled floors added a quiet elegance to the room, while rich shades of red, green, and gold lent a classically extravagant air.

Sam laced his fingers through hers and they

strolled up to the check-in counter. A cute blonde with a better than average set of breasts beamed ir- ritatingly at Sam. An unreasonable surge of jealously barbed through her, leaving her with the irrational desire to tell the blonde that she'd just had fantastic, gritty sex in a convenience store bathroom off I-40 with the very man she didn't have the tact to covertly ogle.

"Welcome back, Mr. Martelli," she said warmly, the slut. A few efficient keystrokes and then, "Your usual suite, I see." She keyed the cards, then slipped them inside an envelope and slid it across the counter. "Okay. That's got you. Will there be any- thing else?" The hopeful "Like me?" implication hung unspoken in the air.

An altogether too pleased gleam lit his gaze. Sam smiled his thanks, picked the envelope up and tapped it once on the counter. "No, that'll do it."

"Good." She gestured toward a bellman. "An- thony will see you to your suite." The blonde finally deigned to acknowledge Delaney's presence with a cool sweep of her gaze and the look seemed to take her measure and find her unequivocally lacking. "I'm sure you'll enjoy your stay."

Irritation spiked. Delaney smirked, let her gaze lin- ger pointedly on Sam, and said, "I'm sure we will."

Sam chuckled under his breath and guided her to- ward the elevator. "Retract the claws, honey. She's only being friendly."

"Yeah. To you."

Sam laughed, a deep masculine rumble that shivered her insides. The bellman held the elevator door open for them and Sam guided her in with a finger snugged deliciously at the small of her back.

"Yeah, laugh now, you wretch," Delaney said, whacking him playfully on the arm. "But I guarantee you, were the situation reversed, you'd have your claws out as well."

Delaney was pleased to note that a little of the male satisfaction that had clung to his smile faded as he considered what she'd just said. Then it vanished altogether.

"Sorry," he said with a sheepish grin. "Would it be horribly tacky of me to admit that I liked the fact that you seemed to be a little jealous?"

A little jealous? Hell, she'd been a great deal more than a little jealous. She'd been ready to dive over the counter and go for that girl's throat. Completely unreasonable and yet she couldn't seem to help herself.

"Yes, it's tacky," Delaney said primly. She poked her tongue in her cheek and rocked back on her heels. "But no more tacky than me practically smacking a 'taken' sign across your groin," she said drolly. "So you're forgiven."

A strangled laugh erupted from the bellman, reminding Delaney that they weren't alone.

Sam's eyes widened and another laugh rumbled from his chest. "Thank you," he told her, sliding a knuckle across her cheek.

The elevator drew to a smooth stop on the tenth floor. She and Sam followed the bellman down the hall. Seconds later, they were ushered into one of the plushest suites she'd ever seen—and she'd seen many. On the rare occasions Delaney traveled, she did so in style.

This suite had been named after the current owner of the Ravenwood Estate, James Morgan Pierce, and was housed in the turret. A king-size bedroom, spacious living room, dining room, wet bar and pantry were just some of the amenities in the luxuriously appointed set of rooms.

Decorated in shades of pale yellow and light blue, with fine reproduction antique furniture and a bank of curved windows that drew one's feet across the thick cushy carpet, Delaney instantly fell in love with the accommodations. Breathtaking views of the Blue Ridge Mountains were visible from every room, making one feel like part of the landscape. It was aesthetically pleasing, fed the senses, and highly— unquestionably—romantic.

Despite the fact that there was so much to see and do, Delaney came to the abrupt conclusion that staying in the room with him for the duration wouldn't be such a bad plan.

Her gaze drifted to Sam, who'd just tipped the bellman, and a desire erupted, sending little rivers of heat coursing through her blood. He'd just treated her to another one of those chocolate-covered orgasms less than an hour ago, and yet were he to so much as crook his little finger, she'd wrap her legs around his waist again and beg him for another helping. He turned, met her gaze and a ready smile leapt to his lips, making something in her chest alternately tighten and expand.

"This is incredible," she told him.

"I thought you'd like it."

She grinned. "You thought right."

Those gorgeous lips curled into a sexy half smile and he quirked a tentative brow. "Have I thought enough things right for you to let me take a few pictures of you this weekend?"

Delaney smiled and bit her lip. "That depends," she said cautiously. She thought she knew what he had in mind and, surprisingly, she found herself receptive to the idea. Had even packed a few special Laney creations just for the occasion. Another baby step, another little victory, she thought, pleased with her progress.

Humor lightened his dark perceptive gaze. "On what?"

Delaney settled herself into a chaise lounge and toed her shoes off with a grateful sigh. "On what kind of pictures you want to take."

"That's easy enough," he said. "I want to take any kind of picture you're willing to let me."

"Hmm. I'll think about it," she hedged, though a secret thrill had kicked her heart rate up. "So, we're going to grab a bite to eat and then go over and tour the house, right?"

Sam nodded. "Right. I have to shoot the after-rehearsal dinner tonight, and the wedding tomorrow afternoon, but we'll still have plenty of time to do everything else that we'll want to do."

Good, Delaney thought, because in addition to seeing the estate and all it had to offer, she wanted to have plenty of time to do him.

Repeatedly.

SHE HAD THAT LOOK AGAIN, Sam thought. That same come-pump-me look that she'd gotten in the convenience store. Those bright green eyes had gone all soft and dark with desire and she'd bit down on that bottom lip, and he'd known—*known*—that she wanted him.

Right then.

He'd been more than willing to accommodate her then—hell, he'd hauled her into the bathroom and taken her against the damned door—and he was more than willing to accommodate her now, if she were so inclined.

Sam was no stranger to sex and had participated in more than his share of strange sex, particularly in his younger days. He'd made it in a movie theater, in a car—*while driving*—a memorable yet unforgivably stupid act, and he'd even made it one of those little photo booths in the mall.

In more recent years, he liked to think that he'd matured and that his tastes had matured as well. Rather than perfecting the quickie as so many of his male counterparts seemed to enjoy, he'd wanted to perfect drawing out the pleasure. He'd made a game of seeing just how far he could push a partner, just how far he could push himself. He took his time, because in his opinion, half the fun was the anticipation. He considered himself a true hedonist, had a passion for the process of seduction. He enjoyed every aspect of it, from the first kiss—that first mingling of breath—to the final thrust and shudder of ultimate climax.

But one little melting look from this woman and every bit of that practiced, controlled mentality evaporated. He became an unprincipled animal with no thought for anything but seeing how quickly he could plant himself between her thighs. It was madness, sheer madness, and yet somehow—with her—it seemed right.

Being with her in any shape, form or fashion seemed right.

"I'm hungry," Delaney suddenly announced.

Sam laughed at the abrupt statement. "I am, too. Do you want to order room service, or go downstairs?"

"Why don't we go downstairs? I'd rather order room service for breakfast. We'll have time to unpack later, right?"

Sam nodded and thoughtfully stroked his chin. He'd need time to set up his equipment, but so long as they were back by six, he should have plenty of time to get everything in order.

"Yeah, that sounds fine," Sam told her. "I'll have to see to my equipment, then spend a couple of hours downstairs working. After that, we'll have the rest of the evening and, so long as I've got my camera out, I might even snap a few of those pictures I asked you about."

Her eyes twinkled. "Persistent, aren't you?"

"It pays to be persistent...particularly when you know the risk is more than equal to the reward."

Something wicked shifted in her gaze. "Ah, but it also pays to be patient. Patience, after all, is a virtue."

She wasn't so keen on patience when she wanted him a couple of hours ago, but Sam didn't think she'd appreciate that little insight. Still... "Occasionally patience can be overrated."

She arched a humorous brow. "Is that so? Is that merely speculation or a personal observation?"

He offered her a hand up. "It's a personal observation. In fact, I'll bet you that at some point—" hopefully several, Sam thought "—over the course of this weekend, I'll be able to point out an admirable example of that opinion."

The next time he had her begging for release came speedily to mind.

Delaney's small hand grasped his and he pulled her up off the chaise. She landed right up against his chest and, to his immeasurable delight, she didn't retreat so much as an inch. Those lush breasts were enticingly pressed against him and her sweet, floral scent swirled around his head. Heat pooled in his gut, slithered through his groin and goose bumps pebbled his skin.

Her eyes twinkled with a knowing humor. "That sounds like an intriguing wager. Care to make it interesting?"

Uneasiness suddenly camped in the back of his neck. Why did he feel like he'd just sprung some sort of trap? Still, he knew better than to show any fear. "Sure. What do you have in mind?"

"I bet that I can point it out first."

He drew back a smidge. "So you agree with me, then?"

"Yes. I never disagreed with you." Her eyes twinkled. "I just think that I'll be able to point it out first."

In other words, Sam thought, she intended to make *him* beg first. Well, that was certainly a challenge he couldn't resist. Clearly, she didn't know whom she was dealing with. Fine. He would teach her a lesson they both would enjoy.

"And if you don't?"

"If I don't, then you get to make those pictures you were talking about."

"And if you do?"

That wicked element he'd detected in her gaze infected her smile as well. "If I do, then I get to make a few pictures of *you*."

A disbelieving chuckle bubbled up his throat, and he inwardly blanched at the possibility. "W-what?"

"If I win, then I get to take pictures of you," she repeated with a laugh. A mischievous twinkle danced in her eyes. "*I* get to tell *you* what to wear, where to sit, lay, whatever. And when this weekend is over, that roll of film is mine to keep."

Sam's earlier confidence took a dramatic nose-dive. He'd never been on the other side of the camera, and frankly, the idea didn't appeal to him at all. He didn't know why, precisely. He took good care of himself, made faithful trips to the gym and stayed fit. He'd also never had any problem attracting the opposite sex, so he'd assumed that he had to be somewhat appealing. Though it might sound conceited, he wasn't the least bit concerned with looking bad on film. Furthermore, he didn't have a modest bone in his body.

But he still didn't want to do it.

Go figure. How weird was that? He made his living taking boudoir photos of women—and the occasional gay man—yet when it came right down to it, he apparently didn't have the balls to bare all and get on the other side of the camera. The realization made his gut fill with self-disgust and left him feeling more than a little uneasy.

"Ah…this looks like a case where the shrink could use a little bit of his own therapy." She squeezed his fingers. "What?" she scoffed. "Afraid you'll lose?"

"No," Sam said immediately, because men never

ignored a taunt, bet, or dare. It was against their nature, and most particularly, his.

Still, nothing could be further from the truth. He was afraid he'd lose—lose control—because God knows he didn't seem to have any where this woman was concerned. Then he'd lose the bet, and she'd gleefully take his camera and... And his brain seized. He couldn't wrap his mind around the rest.

"Good," she replied cheerfully. "Then it's a bet."

What? What had he just unwittingly agreed to? Oh, hell. Screw it, Sam thought. In for a penny, in for a pound. He'd just have to make sure that he didn't lose. And he'd start tonight by putting her firmly in her place.

On her back.

In the meantime, he'd settle for something else. He lowered his voice. "It's a bet. Now let's seal it with a kiss."

Sam slanted his lips over hers, gentle yet firm, a kiss designed to mimic sex, promise heaven, weaken her knees and leave her gasping for breath. He loved to kiss her, could feast on this woman's mouth forever and it still wouldn't be long enough. Curiously, when he reluctantly dragged his lips from hers, he could barely stand, could scarcely force air into his lungs.

A premonition, Sam feared, of things to come.

11

THREE HOURS LATER, Sam returned their digital audio equipment at the end of the tour, then laced his fingers through hers and led her out to the coffee shop that had been housed in what used to be the stable area.

Delaney's mind was awhirl with information and images. The opulence and splendor of the estate and its furnishings were beyond her scope of imagination. The design, the intricate architectural details and workmanship, combined with the lavish silk-draped walls, gilded fixtures, priceless art, and turn-of-the-century pieces was almost more than she could take in.

She'd seen things today that she'd only read about in books. Fifteenth-century Flemish tapestries, paintings by Renoir, Whistler and more. Grecian friezes. An eighteenth-century Pellegrini canvas, an ivory chess set that had reportedly belonged to a legendary French emperor. She'd been awed, filled with quiet appreciation and excitement.

Delaney peered at Sam over the rim of her café au lait. And the entire experience had been made all the more enjoyable by being with him. She'd felt his tall presence, equally reassuring and stimulating, alongside her every step of the way. He'd kept a hand at her waist, at the small of her back, or his fingers threaded through hers for the duration, hadn't broken that calmly distracting contact once.

Though he'd been through the tour countless times, his fascination seemed every bit as fresh as hers and he seemed to take great pleasure in simply enjoying her reactions. She'd caught him staring at her with a slightly bemused smile a couple of times and seeing that curiously fascinated look had made the warm tinglies swirl in her belly.

Truth be told, she was enjoying herself entirely too much for comfort, and yet she couldn't seem to help herself. Delaney had considered dredging up the remembered pain and humiliation of recent events—knew she should use it to keep from making another potential error—but no matter how many times she mentally chanted men-sucked, baby-steps, little-victories, she couldn't seem to work up any real indignation or enthusiasm for the process.

She *liked* Sam Martelli.

Swearing off men in general seemed like a good, sensible plan in theory, but keeping that mentality when faced with a guy like him—a guy who made her heart stumble and her panties wet—well, that was a completely different story.

Delaney wasn't foolish enough to let herself fall in love with him—she knew better than that. But she had fallen seriously in *like* with him and planned to take advantage of this dream weekend he'd given her. This weekend was about fun and sex—nothing else. No sticky emotions, no wistful if-onlys or what-ifs.

She wouldn't allow it.

This man, for whatever reason, tempted her out of her comfort zone, made her momentarily forget her insecurities. She forgot about that mocked fat child, forgot about the pain of being a misfit, of not being perfect, because, against all reason, she felt perfect with him. Furthermore, he enticed her into doing all the wicked, wonderful things she'd always dreamed of doing—the very things that inspired her lingerie—but that she'd never had the guts to try, or the right partner to try them with.

She'd funneled every bit of that sexual energy into her work, into a safe unemotional outlet. Why had she done that? Delaney wondered now. What had made her put everything she had into her work, with-out leaving anything left over for herself? Was it her modesty issues, or had something else been the cause? She didn't know. But she was grimly deter-mined to find out.

With him.

With every second she spent with him, she could feel herself swiftly growing less guarded and more wickedly confident. More comfortable in her own skin. For whatever reason, he seemed to be the an-tidote to her modesty and she firmly intended to have him inject her with as much of the wonder drug as possible. After all, he certainly possessed a fine…syringe.

"Have I missed something?" Sam asked.

Delaney blinked. "No. Why?"

His eyes twinkled. "Because that grin you're wearing looks a little…lurid."

Delaney felt a blush stain her cheeks, thankful that he wasn't privy to her ridiculous medical metaphoric musings. "Sorry," she mumbled. "I was woolgathering."

Sam gave her a slightly bemused, probing look, and when it didn't readily reveal anything, he blew out a small breath. "So what was your favorite part of the house?"

Delaney smiled, grateful for the change in subject, and absently swirled a stir stick around her drink. "Oh, I don't know," she sighed. "I don't know if I can pick a favorite part. Every bit of it was wonderful."

"Still," he insisted lightly. "There has to be a favorite room, a favorite piece." He licked a little whipped cream from his mocha.

"Well," Delaney hedged, suddenly mesmerized by the way his tongue lazily lapped at his drink. She instantly imagined it licking her in woefully neglected places. "If I had to pick—"

"You do," Sam interjected matter-of-factly. His dark eyes twinkled. "It's part of a little thing I like to call *post-tour etiquette*."

Delaney chuckled, though a tense heat had begun

to wind its way through her body. "Well, in that case…I suppose the library would have to be my favorite."

Sam leaned back in his chair and grinned knowingly. "I thought as much. Why?"

She lifted her shoulders in a halfhearted shrug. "Because it served more of a purpose than simply being beautiful."

And it was beautiful. Two stories, a muraled ceiling, huge fireplace and carved walnut bookcases that were works of art in and of themselves. Still…

"Over ten-thousand books, in more than eight different languages," she told him, her voice quietly intense. "Think of the knowledge in that one room. Consider the time and energy that went into each of those books, then the passion behind amassing such a collection." Delaney sagged against the back of her seat and a sigh of admiration slipped between her lips. Her gaze tangled with his. "Someone loved that room. Truly loved it. It's the heart of the house."

Sam wore another one of those curiously bemused looks, not easily read, and a smile gradually worked its way across his lips. "I agree," he murmured.

"What about you?" Delaney asked brightly, in an effort to lighten the moment. Something strange had just passed between them, an altogether too intense something that didn't belong in her plans for the weekend. "What's your favorite room?"

He laughed, shifted back into his chair. "That should be a no-brainer."

Realization dawned. "Ah," Delaney said knowingly. "The Billiards Room."

That slumberous, heavy-lidded gaze twinkled.
"That would be correct."

She rolled her eyes, heaved a put-upon breath.
"Why am I not surprised?"

"Hey, that room is awesome," Sam said, obviously compelled to defend his opinion. "The walls
are covered in hand-tooled Spanish leather, and the
plasterwork on the ceiling is incredible. Not to mention that huge fireplace and that gorgeous old hu-
midor." He nodded indignantly. "There's a lot of
character in that room."

Delaney harrumphed. "Be that as it may, the only
reason you think that room is awesome is because
no women were allowed in there."

He'd readied his mouth for a defensive retort, but
couldn't pull it off. Instead, he quirked a brow and
offered her a slightly repentant grin. "There is that,"
he conceded. "Shallow, huh?"

Delaney chuckled. "Mildly, yes."

His eyes widened in mock astonishment. "Only
mildly. Wow. I thought for sure I'd get roasted for
my beastly sexist opinion."

She lifted one shoulder in a shrug. "There are
feminine touches throughout the rest of the house—
it's the only room out of two-hundred and seventy-
five that's completely masculine. It's only natural
that you like it best." She paused, injected a note of

grim sarcasm into her voice. "It's probably *every* man's favorite room."

Sam winced dramatically and rubbed his jaw. His eyes sparkled with laughter. "Ouch. That was a nice compliment…until you backhanded me with it."

"What can I say?" She chuckled. "I just expected more originality."

"Ouch again," he said with an outraged, semi-wounded laugh. "So now I've lost points for originality?"

Delaney lifted her shoulders in an exaggerated shrug and offered him a tiny smile. "Sorry."

Suddenly, a promising gleam underscored the humor in those gorgeous bedroom eyes, and his smile turned almost…predatory. "Well, I'll just have see about earning those points back, won't I?" He lapped at his mocha again, gazed at her over the rim. "Redeem myself, so to speak."

Oy. If earning those points back lived up to the innuendo in that sexy rasp, she'd undoubtedly end up giving him an award for ingenuity.

That playfully intense gaze tangled with hers. "After all, I have no desire to disappoint you. I'm only interested in your complete satisfaction."

Sweet heaven, the temperature around their table had suddenly spiked. Delaney resisted the urge to fan herself. "That's reassuring," she managed, despite the sudden flash of warmth burning the tops of her thighs. "I have a vested interest in my satisfaction."

"So do I," she thought she heard him murmur, and his voice held a curiously grim element.

Delaney blinked. "I'm sorry?"

His expression cleared and he abruptly checked his watch, then the corner of his mouth tucked into a tsk of regret. "I hate to do this, but I've got to get back to the hotel and set up. Do you want to stay here and do a little more exploring, or would you like to catch a shuttle with me?"

Fatigue settled in her shoulders. Between the long drive and the excitement of the house, she'd about run out of get-up-and-go. Sam had said he'd be gone for a couple of hours. That would give her time to take a bath and a much-needed nap. She had a feeling that she was going to need every bit of energy she could muster for tonight, particularly in light of Sam's recent quest to reclaim his originality points.

Mercy, she hoped she survived it...but she looked forward to trying.

SAM FINISHED THE SET-UP for tomorrow afternoon's photos, bid the happy couple good-night, then slung his camera bag over his shoulder and headed back upstairs to join Delaney.

Just the thought of her made his lips slide into a grin, made his step quicken in anticipation, made his groin tight with unequalled lust. The trip through the estate this afternoon had been a major revelation, one that inspired a great deal more confidence in the relationship he'd almost blindly decided to build.

Even without the "quickening"—after this weekend—Sam knew without a shadow of a doubt that he would have recognized her as the one for him.

Delaney Walker simply got it. Got him.

If he looked from now until the end of time, he knew he'd never find another female who suited him any better.

Delaney's tastes mirrored his own, they thought along the same lines, appreciated the same things. The more time he spent with her, the more he felt the connection, felt the vibe.

For lack of a better description, they were attuned to one another. For instance, he didn't have to look to know where she was, he could *feel* her. Could sense her, like radar. And, while he couldn't read her mind—though she'd laughingly accused him of that very thing earlier today—he did seem to possess the uncanny ability to anticipate her thoughts and actions. To know what she wanted, when she wanted it, and react accordingly.

A frown pulled at his lips. Regrettably, he still sensed that she didn't want *him.* Not permanently, anyway. She wanted this weekend—wanted sex—but as far as really wanting him—nada, nothing, zilch. The idea inspired no small amount of panic, made his belly twist with anxiety. With any other woman, this attitude would have been like a dream come true. Guiltless sex? What man didn't want that? Men and women had been at odds over it for centuries. Men wanted sex with no commitment.

Women wanted a commitment before sex. It was the perfect form of irony.

Just his luck he'd finally meet a woman he wanted a forever with and, in exchange for his heart, she wanted to borrow his dick for the weekend. It was damned disturbing. And to top things off, just when he'd begun to make a little headway with her, he'd had to give up his advantage and go to work.

Hell, who knew what she was thinking about now? She'd had hours up there alone. Hours to think all sorts of wrong-headed thoughts. To eat chocolate and think men sucked. And he wanted her to think about him, dammit. Sam boarded the elevator and pressed the button for the tenth floor. He wanted her to think about his hands on her body, his mouth on her breast, and his rod rooted firmly between her thighs. He wanted her to think about him as a potential husband, as a father. He wanted her to think about rocking chairs and grandchildren. He wanted her to think about making him a part of her life.

Sam expelled a heavy breath. Right now she only wanted him in her bed and he supposed that was as good a place as any to start. She'd agreed to come with him, and he knew that had been no small decision on her part. It had been a tremendous step in the right direction. Now if only he could convince her that he didn't want to be just a weekend lover— he wanted to be her *last* and only lover. More importantly, he wanted her to reciprocate the sentiment.

Sam exited the elevator and made his way down

the long wide hall to their suite. He knocked lightly and, when she didn't readily come to the door, he fished his keycard out and planted it in the lock, then quietly let himself in. The living room was empty, however a low light shone from the bedroom. Sam moved silently across the carpet to the bedroom and leaned against the doorjamb. His lips slid into a slow grin and a curious sensation commenced in his chest.

Delaney was fast asleep on top of the comforter, her head pillowed on her arm. Soft light from the bedside lamp bathed her face in a golden glow, picked up the slivery shimmer in her silky moonbeam hair. Long lashes painted shadowed crescents on her cheeks and there was something so heartbreakingly beautiful, so utterly vulnerable about her that he could scarcely draw in a breath. His chest had grown inexplicably tight and his throat had clogged with some nebulous obstruction. Every hair on his body had prickled again and his rod had instantly swelled to full mast.

She wore a short red satin robe that ended around mid-thigh and the sash had loosened sometime during her nap, leaving a deep V of smooth skin open to his gaze. The silky material had gapped enticingly above her waist, exposing one creamy breast and a smooth flat belly. A pair of barely-there red-laced panties embroidered with tiny little pearls hugged her mound, arched up over her wonderful hips in a seductive curve. Every inch of her skin was smooth, glowed with health, and Sam was suddenly hit with the almost irrepressible urge to slide his hands all over her sweetly shaped form, to learn each and every contour and curve, read her body like Braille.

He was also hit with another almost irrepressible urge—shutterbug fever. He mentally framed a few shots and felt his fingers twitch in response. She looked absolutely amazing, so damned sexy. If only she could see herself like this, Sam thought. If she could see herself the way *he* saw her, would she still feel modest and self-conscious? he wondered. Would she be embarrassed…or pleasantly surprised? Sam sucked in a breath through his teeth as indecision plagued him.

Taking pictures of her without her knowledge seemed a little voyeuristic, made him feel a bit like a dirty old man, but he found himself unable to resist the temptation and he instinctively reached for his camera. Just a few shots, Sam thought, taking care to be as quiet as possible. Just a few shots and, if they were half as gorgeous as he thought they would be, he'd give them to her as a surprise. He only hoped it was a surprise she'd appreciate.

He fired off a couple of full lengths and one heart-stoppingly beautiful headshot, then moved in for a close-up. He'd just pulled her face into focus when those bright green eyes opened and blinked sleepily at him through his lens.

Her lips curled into a tender smile. "Hey," she said, her voice slightly rusty.

Sam hadn't realized he'd been holding his breath

until it left him in a relieved whoosh. He pulled the camera away from his face. "Hey, yourself," he said warmly.

Her brow folded in sleepy perplexity. "What are you doing?"

"Being sneaky," he admitted sheepishly.

She chuckled, stretched lightly, causing her breast to play hide-and-seek beneath the silky fabric. "I noticed that," she said with a slow quirk of her brow. "How many pictures did you take before I woke up?"

"A few," Sam said, and breathed a tentative sigh of relief. Surely if she were going to get pissed, she'd erupt immediately, not lie in wait for him like a dormant volcano. Furthermore—astonishingly—she seemed completely oblivious to the fact that she was practically naked and the room wasn't pitch-black.

He, however, was *not* oblivious.

All of that naked skin was wreaking havoc with his senses, causing a riot in his groin. His skin had grown inexplicably hot, his breath came in tentative shallow puffs and he'd hardened to the point just short of pain. Were that not enough, gooseflesh raced up and down his spine and an odd tingling had settled in his neck. Need lashed through him, whipped at his nerve endings.

A sparkle of humor danced in her eyes and she tsked groggily. "Didn't anyone ever tell you that taking pictures of someone while they were sleeping—

and without their consent—was rude, Martelli? What happened to your manners?'' she accused playfully.

"Sorry...but you're gorgeous. I couldn't resist." He gave her a hopeful grin. "I, uh, don't suppose you'd let me take a few more?"

"Expecting that persistence to pay off?"

Sam grinned. "Er...hoping would be more accurate. Come on," he cajoled softly. "Just a few. You don't even have to move. Just lie there."

Another sexy chuckle bubbled up her throat and her eyes twinkled merrily. "What?" she asked in mock bewilderment. "Did we get married and I forgot?"

Sam sucked in his cheeks and cast her an amused glance. "That didn't come out exactly right, did it?"

She cocked her head. "Er...no."

"But you know what I mean. What do you say?" He took a chance and let his gaze suggestively roam the length of her, lowered his voice to more intimate level. "You look sexy as hell."

Her breath momentarily hitched, but luckily she neither froze, nor darted for cover. "I do?"

Need broadsided him. Made his mouth alternately dry then water. "Like an exquisite gift loosely wrapped in red satin." He fingered the hem. "One of yours?"

She nodded.

"It's hot." So hot he wanted to carefully peel it off her, then taste every place that the fabric had been. "Let me take a few shots," he repeated softly.

Her mouth formed a wobbly smile, and at last she gave him a what-the-hell nod. Sam inwardly breathed a sigh of relief. He lifted his camera once more, pulled that perfect body into focus.

"Do you have any idea how much I want you right now?" he asked her, his voice husky even to his own ears. He didn't know where the words were coming from, but instinctively knew they were the right ones to say. "Any idea at all?"

Her lips curled wickedly. "That tent in the front of your slacks is a pretty good indicator."

His brows rose and a smile claimed his lips. "There is that." He bent down on one knee and pulled an amazing frame into focus. "But there are physical indicators that you want me just as much," he murmured silkily.

"Oh?"

Sam nodded.

"Like what?" she asked. A spark of something naughty flashed in her gaze.

He lowered his voice a notch. "Well, for starters, you've got that look in your eye, that soft, melted, I-want-you-now look. You've bit your bottom lip a couple of times, another provocatively telling gesture—it means you want me to taste you—and, most noticeably—" Sam's gaze dropped to that one gloriously bare breast and lingered hungrily "—your nipples have budded, anticipating my touch, waiting for my kiss."

Delaney's bright green gaze darkened to a velvety

emerald and had taken on a distinctly slumberous quality. Her tongue peeked out and licked her luscious bottom lip. With a soft sigh, she rolled over onto her back and smoothed her hand down her belly, an intensely erotic movement that made Sam's dick jerk hard against his briefs. His heart stuttered. Oh, this was too good to miss. He refocused, pulled the entire picture into his lens, captured the moment on film.

She hummed a low note of approval. "Guess what?"

"What?"

"There are other parts of my body that are anticipating your touch," Delaney whispered huskily.

She cast him a sexy sidelong glance, one that held a gleam of recklessness, a combination of boldness and nerve that he'd never seen before. This sensual rose was blooming right before his eyes, unfurling petal by petal.

Blooming…just for him.

And he didn't plan to miss a single minute of it.

12

SAM SWALLOWED THICKLY, took up his camera once more. "Is that right?"

"That's right," she purred, shifting languorously. Her hair slithered over her shoulders.

"Which parts would those be?"

Delaney slid both hands back up over her belly, over her rib cage and gently cupped her breasts. "These parts," she murmured breathlessly.

Sam had never seen anything so gorgeously erotic in his entire life. He sucked in a harsh breath and continued to snap shots in quick succession, moved to capture different angles.

"What other parts?" he asked through his constricted throat.

She plumped her breasts in her hands, widening the gap in her robe, revealing more of her delectable body to his greedy gaze. She flicked her thumbs over her distended nipples and her eyes fluttered gently shut beneath the weight of sensation. Her mouth opened in a silent moan of satisfaction. "Th-these parts," she breathed.

There was something so incredibly beautiful about a woman's hands roaming wantonly over her body,

Sam thought as he systematically framed several more pictures. His pulse roared in his ears, which was an absolute miracle, because he wouldn't have thought there'd be enough blood left in the head on his shoulders to hear it—the majority of it had flooded his groin, giving him the most torturous erection he'd ever had. Gooseflesh wracked his body, resulting in a violent shiver.

This entire scene was beyond surreal, exceeded his limit of understanding. Seeing a woman touch herself in such an intimate way made a man wonder how she would touch him. How those selfsame hands would feel shaping his body, sliding up and down his swollen rod. What other carnal pleasures could those small feminine hands accomplish?

"I love your parts, baby," Sam choked out unsteadily as Delaney rolled her nipples between her fingers. "Are there any others that you want to tell me about? Any others that need my attention?"

She raked her teeth over her bottom lip and her eyes glittered with undisguised longing. "There's one part, in particular, that needs your attention." Her voice was a needy, sultry purr.

One hand played idly at her breast, while the other smoothed down her middle over her gently curved abdomen. Her fingers brushed the top of her lacy panties, slid over her mound and dallied between her thighs. She winced with pleasure, squirmed languidly and leisurely stroked her clever fingers over the silky scrap of fabric snugged against her sex.

Sam's typically steady fingers trembled on the shutter button, and beads of sweat gathered on his upper lip. His entire body had grown tight with tension, locked rigid with need. He'd reached the outermost limits of his control. He framed a couple more shots—unable to control the impulse—but certainly not to preserve the memory. Hell, he didn't need a picture for that. The erotic stepped-from-his-fantasies vision she made right now would be permanently, indelibly imprinted in his brain.

"Sam?" Her hot gaze found his. "Are you going to play with that camera all night…or are you going to play with me?" She slipped a finger beneath the thong, forcing a single bead of moisture from his engorged rod.

Oh, he'd play with her all right, Sam thought, unnaturally calm given the desperate need he felt licking hotly through his singed veins. He set the camera aside, tugged his shirt free of his pants and swiftly removed the buttons from their closures. He'd had several lovers who enjoyed undressing him, had always enjoyed it as well, but he discovered that having a woman stare at him while he undressed—having her greedy gaze watch and catalogue his every move—was equally enjoyable.

Particularly when that woman was all but naked and needy, when her fingers were playing lazily beneath her panties.

A surge of lust powered through him, causing a slight tremor in his fingers. He shrugged out of his shirt and let it fall carelessly to the floor. Seconds later his pants and briefs joined the forgotten pile, then he stalked naked toward the bed.

Delaney's fevered gaze did a slow head-to-toe inspection, then lingered pointedly—longingly—on his groin. She licked her lips once more. Though he would have thought it impossible, his rod swelled even more, jerked toward her. Her eyes glittered with hungry anticipation and her mouth curled into a knowing curve.

"I'm ready to play," he whispered silkily as he crawled onto the bed beside her. He slid one long, deliberate finger between her breasts, down her belly, and over her mound. "Where would you like me to start?"

She shivered delicately and her breath hitched. Her heavy-lidded gaze tangled with his and she lifted one small shoulder in a semblance of a shrug. "Surprise me."

A laugh stuttered out of him and his customary confidence momentarily wavered. Surprise her? How? What did she want? Clearly she expected something spectacular tonight, something beyond the typical carnal pleasures. She'd bloomed for him, shed a lifetime of insecurities and expected to be rewarded accordingly for her effort.

The weight of her expectations settled in Sam's chest, pushing a silent sigh from his lips. Every moment spent with her had been important—had been an integral part of making her his—but for reasons which escaped him, he knew that the next few hours spent in this bed were fundamentally key, would ultimately either make or break him as far as Delaney was concerned. Sam swallowed an ironic laugh.

He literally couldn't afford to screw up.

The conclusion was damned intimidating and didn't facilitate the seduction process whatsoever. Luckily, his body seemed to know what to do. Rather than put a great deal of thought into the act, Sam simply let impulse take over. Ceded control to his baser instincts.

He swallowed a shallow breath, traced a reverent half moon over her cheek, then bent down and brushed his lips gently over each of her lids, then along the smooth curve of her brow, and over the gentle slope of her cheek.

Thankfully her breath trembled past her lips in silent confirmation of this tactic, and a tad of tension wilted out of his spine.

He skimmed his lips lightly over hers in the merest touch and inwardly melted with relief as he savored her resulting sigh. She smoothed one hand along his upper arm, over his neck, and then threaded her fingers through the hair at his nape. Chills pebbled his skin and he deepened the kiss by imperceptible degrees until their bodies and tongues were mindlessly tangled around each other in a hot, mad pursuit of hedonistic pleasures. Within seconds, he'd removed her robe and panties, shoved them off the bed.

He couldn't taste enough of her, couldn't satisfy

the hunger for her skin. Her sweet smell assaulted his senses, made him breathe deeply of her. He kissed, licked and laved every part of her—her neck, her shoulders, her breasts, and her belly—and his breath hissed past his teeth as she treated him to the same pleasant torture. Her hands mapped his body, moved greedily over his burning flesh as though addicted to the feel of him.

"You're gorgeous," Delaney said as she skimmed her nails over his chest, scored lightly over his nipples. Her gaze was all soft, her pupils dilated with desire. A flush of heat pinkened her silken skin. "I love touching you, tasting you. In fact, I'd like to taste you—" she wrapped one hand around his throbbing rod "—here, while you taste me—" she reached down and brushed her fingers over her drenched curls "—there."

Sweet heaven. His mouth watered at the thought and he swiftly moved to accommodate her. Sam parted her curls at the precise instant that she grasped his rod and ran her hot tongue over the engorged head. An involuntary shiver gripped him, and he set his jaw against the exquisite sensation, then reciprocated the gesture in kind. He laved her swollen clit, shaped his tongue around the sensitized nub and licked greedily. Thighs quivering, Delaney bucked off the sheet, then tongued him from root to tip. Sam groaned, and parlayed the response by blowing a steady stream of air against her pink flesh, then fastening his mouth over her and sucking gently.

A whimper broke over his rod as she continued her sweet, mind-wrecking assault. She curled her tongue around him, nibbled along his length, then grasped the base of his rod and took him fully into her hot mouth. Sam's muscles locked, his thighs tensed and he grew impossibly more hungry for her. He hovered on the brink of release, yet he still lapped at her, fed and suckled, worked her hooded nub against his tongue.

For his every move, she countered with one equally provocative, equally arousing, equally frantic. He could feel her trembling beneath him, could feel the tension building with each hard sweep of his tongue, could feel the same intensity building steadily inside him, yet he was powerless to stop it. Didn't want to. Her musky scent curled around his nostrils and she tasted so damned sweet, and he wanted to be there between her thighs when she came, wanted to lap up every ounce of her release.

The thought was no sooner born than Delaney bucked violently beneath him, simultaneously climaxed and sucked him hard into her mouth. He came, blasted his seed against the back of her throat, even as he drank deeply between her legs, savored the sweet, salty taste of her release against his tongue. She licked him, milked him dry and heaved a contented sigh of sublime satisfaction.

Sam had never in his life experienced anything so erotic, so incredible. His thighs and insides still trembled. Every cell in his body had weakened with the force of release. He lapped at her a final time, then turned and caught her pleased, cat-in-the-cream expression.

"Now, *that* was a very good surprise," she said meaningfully.

"You know I won the bet, so you have to do what I say," Delaney insisted hours later with no small amount of wicked satisfaction. "That was the deal. Now take it off."

"Delaney," Sam said warningly. His nostrils flared and color flagged his cheeks. He looked immensely uncomfortable.

"Honestly, I don't know why you bothered putting your briefs back on." She gave them a skeptical look. "No offense, but plain serviceable white isn't conducive to the sexy layout I have in mind." She bit her lip consideringly. "Now if you were wearing a pair of black silk boxers with red chili peppers on them, then that would be different." Lucky for her, he wasn't. She wanted him naked. "But since you aren't—" she manufactured a regretful smile "—then they'll need to come off."

His gaze twinkled with perceptive humor. "You are really enjoying this, aren't you?"

She nodded. "Yes. Yes, I am."

"Fine," Sam said at last. He reluctantly stood and stripped his underwear off. "Now what?"

Delaney feasted on the sight of him. All of that splendidly proportioned muscle, all that strength and virility had been hers to play with tonight. To explore. Her skin tingled and her pulse beat warmly at her center, bringing to mind the countless orgasms she'd been privy to this evening.

They'd made love in every imaginable position—in some that were plain unimaginable—and had christened every room in the suite. They'd made it in the bed, in the shower, on the sofa, and on the dining room table. He'd stretched her naked body out on the carpet in front of the bank of windows, had let the moonlight kiss her skin and forced her to look at herself in the throes of complete, mindless passion.

Delaney had been amazed at what she'd seen, had been awed at the sight of their joined bodies, at the sight of her own body reflected in the glass. Granted she didn't have a model-perfect body, but that hadn't mattered because he clearly hadn't seen any flaws. He'd gazed at her as though she were the most gorgeous woman in the world, had devoured her with those dark, hungry eyes. Who could be self-conscious, would even have time to be, with a man like Sam Martelli positioned deeply between their thighs?

Delaney swallowed, forced her thoughts back to the task at hand. "Why don't you lay on the bed?" she drawled suggestively. "Pick a comfortable position." Her gaze bumped into his. "A pose that's natural to you."

Predictably, he recognized his own directives and smiled. "You have a good memory."

"I'm also pretty good with a camera." Impatience thrummed through her. "Assume the position. I'm ready to start."

His lips quirked into a smoldering, droll smile. "Want me to straighten the sheets out first?"

"No," she murmured. "I like the idea of you and rumpled sheets."

That grin flashed again, the one that made her knees weak and her tummy clench. "Okay," he said slowly, and crawled onto the bed.

His muscles bulged and rippled invitingly and his penis swelled between his legs in semi-arousal, laid against one heavily muscled thigh. His big, hard, tanned body sprawled negligently in those white, tangled sheets was a sight to behold. His hair lay in dark, mussed waves and those sinfully dark, heavy-lidded eyes glittered with sexy humor.

Delaney's gaze lingered on that handsome face, marveled over the even, remarkably formed countenance and something achy shifted in her chest, some nameless horrifying emotion that didn't belong on this trip, in this bedroom, or God forbid, in her heart.

She hid her face behind the camera lest he recognize the sentiment and, with a shaky breath, carefully pulled the frame into focus. She took several shots, then lowered the camera.

"You can move, you know."

He grimaced. "You said for me to get comfortable. I'm comfortable."

Her lips curled. "Okay, now I'm telling you to find another *comfortable* position."

"Damn," he grumbled. "How many times am I going to have to do this?"

"That depends."

"On what?" he asked warily.

She smiled sweetly. "On how many exposures are on this roll of film."

He uttered a hot oath, pushed a hand through his hair. "Then that would be thirty-six minus the three you just took."

"Get busy," she instructed.

His lids drifted to half-mast and he caught his full bottom lip with his teeth and slowly released it. Sexual heat rolled off him, burning her up from the inside out. "Wouldn't my time be better spent *surprising* you?"

Mercy. That was certainly a tempting scenario. Still… "You can do that right now," Delaney told him. "Surprise me now."

A frustrated sigh blew past his lips, even as they curled with the promise of untold pleasure. "Put that camera down, come here, and I'll surprise you until your eyes roll back in your head," he said heatedly. "I swear."

Her knees quaked. "Make me," Delaney taunted.

"How?" he all but wailed.

She lowered her voice. "The same way I made you."

His eyes rounded and then a deep, wicked chuckle rumbled from his chest. "Oh, you are so…"

"Bad?" she supplied helpfully.

"No. Mean," he said.

She cocked her head. "You didn't seem to think it was mean when you were on the other side of the camera," she told him. "In fact, you seemed to be enjoying yourself tremendously."

"I did," he admitted, his gaze instantly hot once more. "More than you can—"

"So what's the problem?" She lifted the camera. "Which of *your* parts needs *my* attention?"

With a strangled laugh, he grasped his rod. "This one."

She snapped the picture a mere nanosecond before his shocked expression could ruin the frame. "Delaney!" he gasped, clearly horrified.

She burst into unrepressed laughter. "What? You knew the deal when we made the bet."

His mouth gaped. "I didn't real—"

"Stroke it again, baby," she told him. She lowered her voice to a husky rasp. "I want to watch you get hard. It's very…arousing. Makes me all hot and wet."

He swallowed, once, twice, then with a groan of helpless defeat, took himself back in hand. That steely gaze slammed into hers, refused to waver. Delaney's tongue darted out and touched the middle of her upper lip as the intensity, the sheer eroticism of what she was seeing developed fully in her lust-ridden mind.

Six and one-half feet of naked, dark—aroused—male.

He absently stroked himself, yet she knew it was her own hand he felt there, knew that he was imagining her palm gliding up and down the smooth, hard length of him. She was ready to make that vision a reality. Delaney's breath came short and sharp and her skin prickled with want. Her breasts grew impossibly heavy and a heady weight settled in her achy womb.

She snapped a couple more frames, just to save face, then set the camera aside and scaled his body until she settled her weeping sex along the long hard ridge of him. His engorged head bumped her swollen clit, eliciting a broken sigh of need. Heat lashed through her, parched her mouth, then made it water.

Sam's hands bracketed her hips and a wicked smile coupled with the depraved gleam in his eyes made warmth flutter below her navel. He rocked against her folds, sliding up and down her swollen nether lips. His lids fluttered shut and his neck arched. "God, you feel good."

Delaney rocked against him, bit her lip, too, in an effort to stem the flow of pleasure, but she might as well try to bottle wind. It was no use. He felt too good between her legs, too intense. "So do you," she told him.

Unable to stand the emptiness any longer, she repositioned her hips and slowly sank down on top of him. He filled her so completely, it pushed the very air from her lungs, seemingly deflating her. She clamped her muscles around him, then lifted up, dragging the silken skin along with her, then slowly impaled herself on him once more.

"Christ," Sam said through clenched teeth. "You're killing me."

She did it again and again, and remarkably, he let her, didn't try to change her pace, or take over completely. He let her set the rhythm and take him along for the ride.

Smiling with lazy sensuality, he reached up and tweaked her breasts, then when that wasn't enough, he leaned forward and latched his greedy mouth around one aching peak, then the other. Pleasure barbed through her as he fed on her nipples, landed a direct hit against her center. Her muscles tightened, and her body bent against the tight bow of beginning release.

Recognizing the impulse, Sam sucked hard once, then reclined once more. He anchored one hand on her hip and the other moved to where their bodies joined. Her blond curls mingled with his darker ones, an incredibly arousing sight, then his fingers moved into the midst of those curls and gently massaged her clit.

Her mouth opened in a silent *O* as an altogether intense sensation commenced deep inside her. Her muscles clenched and quickened, and her hips began to move with frantic precision—up, down, up, down. With every thrust, she could feel the heavy heat flooding her womb, could feel it filling up. Broken sounds tore from her throat and she closed her eyes and whimpered his name. A fever built inside her, hotter and hotter, until finally—blessedly—her womb filled beyond capacity, and the resulting spill broke like a dam through her, bathing her in the tingling rain of release. A long, silent scream issued from her throat and her back bowed tight. Her muscles clenched around his hard length, the contractions harder, more intense than anything she'd ever experienced before.

Before she could revel over it any longer, Sam rolled her off him onto her belly, then hauled her hips up from the mattress and plunged into her from behind. The shock of sensation forced the breath from her lungs as he nudged deep. He plowed into her, his fingers biting into the tender skin of her hips. He plunged repeatedly, powered himself in and out of her, his testicles slapping against her aching flesh.

Impossibly, she felt herself falling toward release again, felt the spiral of heat dragging her further and further down. She squeezed her eyes shut against the sensation, whimpered. She didn't know if she could take any more, then said as much. "Please!" she cried. "Sam, please!"

He pumped hard, smooth controlled thrusts. She heard the change in his breathing, felt his tight rein on control snap and a thrill raced through her. He hammered into her, harder and harder, faster and faster. She automatically stiffened, bracing herself for the impending climax. With a roar of satisfaction, Sam buried himself to the hilt, bent forward and lightly bit her shoulder.

Lights burst behind her lids and she screamed as she came hard. She felt his hot seed bathe the back of her womb, reveled in the feel of him pulsing deep inside of her.

With a sigh of satisfaction, he rolled to the side, taking her with him and making sure that the bulk of his weight landed on the mattress.

"How…was that…for a…surprise?" he asked brokenly as his chest heaved.

Delaney buried her face in the pillow, then turned to look at him. Delight shimmered in every cell. "Most admirable. I look forward to an encore." She winced as he slowly pulled out of her. "Later."

Concern knitted his brow. "Poor baby. Have I worn you out?"

She nodded, still trying to catch her breath. "I wouldn't be opposed to a quick power nap."

Sam smoothed her hair over the pillow and tucked her more firmly against him. A sweet, tender gesture that melted her heart. The combined sensation of his heat at her back and his big, reassuring presence beside her quickly weighted her lids. Pleasure saturated every pore, warmth and happiness cocooned her and a feeling of rightness settled in her limbs.

She could spend the rest of her life nestled in the comfort of his arms, Delaney thought as she drifted off to sleep. Curiously—frighteningly—no mental admonition accompanied the thought.

13

—————

"I'LL BE BACK," Sam said, then pressed a hungry, lingering kiss to her lips.

Her eyes sparkled with warmth. "I'll be waiting. Naked," she added with a saucy wink.

With a shake of his head and a sigh of regret, Sam slowly made his way downstairs. They'd been on the other two tours he'd wanted to share with her, the behind-the-scenes and the rooftop tour, and had strolled through the gardens as well.

Despite little or no sleep, they had still awoken early this morning, ready to spend the day together. Sam had promised her the morning and early afternoon and he'd delivered. They'd had an amazing time. Had talked about everything from sibling rivalry to eighteenth-century antiques. He'd made many discoveries that only confirmed that she was most definitely the one for him.

Not only was she smart, sexy and tenderhearted, she possessed a keen sense of wit and could make him hard with one sexy arch of her brow, she was an incredible listener and, to his unending surprise, had become an instant friend.

He grimly suspected he was in love with her already.

Which wouldn't be such a bad thing if he knew that he could make her love him in return.

Regrettably, he didn't.

And to make matters worse, it would be several hours before he could get back to her and try to make her love him. The idea made his skin itch, made his stomach clench with dread.

He didn't want to wait hours to be with her—he wanted to be with her *every* hour.

He'd made a tremendous amount of progress with her the last couple of days, could feel her drawing closer and closer to him, and he didn't want to give her the time to backslide, to put those substantial defenses back up. He didn't want to give her time to analyze and evaluate what was happening between them. Didn't want to give her the time to take apart their every minute together and dissect it into a meaningless weekend romp. Sam sincerely hoped that she wouldn't do that.

Last night she'd sloughed off her old insecurities, had blossomed for him like an exotic night-blooming rose. With every second that they spent together, he could feel her confidence strengthening, could feel the power of her femininity taking effect. There was a perpetual wicked twinkle in her bright green gaze, a bold gleam that inspired equal parts anticipation and fear. What in God's name would she think of next? he wondered and prayed he would be up for it.

Sam's cheeks blazed with remembered heat as his late-night photo session leapt graphically to mind. All she'd had to do was tell him that she wanted to watch him get hard, and he'd laid there and stroked himself like a cheap porn star. Let her make pictures of him while he did it, for pity's sake.

She'd calmly pocketed that roll of film this morning, had shot him an I-dare-you look that promised retribution if the film came up missing. He couldn't deny that the whole concept petrified him. He'd asked her to let him develop the film and she'd maddeningly shook her head. She didn't want to run the risk of having them overdeveloped, or inadvertently ruined, she'd told him, the perceptive wench. Sam's lips curled.

That had been precisely what he'd been thinking.

In the event that they were as embarrassing as he thought they would be, he would have cheerfully had a little accident in the darkroom. She'd deftly foiled that plan, Sam thought, unreasonably impressed.

Still, it had occurred to him that she hadn't been the only one testing their limits and stretching their boundaries last night. She'd made him broaden his scope as well. The pictures had only been the tip of the iceberg. She'd made him lose control so many times, had made him completely forget everything in his bag of sexual tricks and act totally on instinct.

He'd lost it repeatedly—hence how she ended up winning the bet and taking the damned pictures.

Were that not disturbing enough, he'd forgotten to protect them that last time. She'd set that camera aside, climbed up his body, then she'd settled that wet part of her against him and every practical thought had fragmented. The singularly intense sensation had been too much for him to handle. Gooseflesh had peppered his skin, every hair on his body had stood on end, and the next thing he'd felt was her hot velvety channel slowly enveloping his inflamed rod. Then he'd ceased thinking at all and had simply felt. The intimate skin-to-skin contact had ripped the breath from his lungs, had made him all but come right that second.

Sam had never had unprotected sex.

Ever.

His parents had pounded the risks and repercussions into his head from the moment he'd been old enough to get an erection, and he'd been suitably wary enough not to disobey them.

He'd always, without hesitation, protected himself and his partner.

The fact that he'd been so caught up in the fever of desire and he hadn't thought to pause and sheath himself in a condom was somehow more telling than any amount of gooseflesh and curious tingling behind his navel. More telling than any Martelli "quickening." This woman had some sort of power over him, had the ability to hold him enthralled. For all intents and purposes—whether she wanted it or not—she had his heart.

He sincerely hoped she didn't break it.

DELANEY SANK INTO A HOT bubble bath and sighed with satisfaction as the warm fragrant water worked its magic and soothed her tender muscles. She and Sam had showered together this morning and, while she'd certainly been soaped up and washed clean, the slippery bath gel had been more of an erotic tool than anything else. Delaney smiled with remembered pleasure, shivered as she mentally relived the frantic slide of his skin against hers, relived the sensation of him embedded deep inside her.

She'd drawn this bath to relax and to think and, just like she'd assumed, her musings were X-rated and all centered on one darkly handsome, tall sexy Italian.

Sam Martelli.

His very name made something clench deep inside her, evoked a strong feeling of contentedness. She longed for a pad and pencil, wanted to doodle his name like some ponytailed grade-school girl under the influence of her first real crush. Her lips curled.

And why not? Delaney wondered. This had certainly been a week for firsts, particularly this weekend. She felt new, fresh. Like a mythological phoenix she felt like she'd been reborn this week and had come out all the better for it.

Delaney didn't have any idea what had happened

exactly, didn't know whether her feelings were a result of her new attitude, of her revenge therapy, or the result of a weekend spent lolling around in hedonistic splendor with a man that secret fantasies were made of.

Probably a combination of all three, but she figured that most of the credit was due to Sam. She couldn't have done this with any other man, she knew. Couldn't have simply let go of old issues and embraced her sensuality. For reasons which escaped her now, he held the key. The feelings he engendered couldn't be reproduced or manufactured with any other man.

Just him.

She knew it as well as she knew her own name. Knew it like she knew the sun would come up in the east and set in the west. She'd denied it every step of the way, had dug her heels in and refused to let emotion play any part of this weekend. Had told herself repeatedly that she wouldn't allow herself to become emotionally invested and, even for a while, she'd managed to make herself believe it.

But regardless of how well she thought she'd protected her heart, she obviously hadn't because she grimly suspected she'd inadvertently—recklessly—pinned it on her sleeve.

His for the plucking, should he be so inclined.

Delaney tried to muster the requisite self-disgust and loathing this monumentally stupid realization should have sparked, but found herself curiously unable to work up any of those feelings.

She was too damned happy.

Yes, she was 0 for 2 in the game of love. Yes, she'd always been a loser magnet and yes, when it came to picking a man who was able to keep his pecker in his pants, show her even a modicum of respect and who didn't have any ulterior motive, she hadn't been very successful. Hadn't been lucky.

But she instinctively knew her luck had just changed.

None of those men were Sam Martelli.

Sam was simply a what-you-see-is-what-you-get kind of guy. She hadn't detected even the smallest hint of dishonesty in his character, not a single red flag had gone up. In her previous relationships, those warnings had sounded and she'd ignored them because she'd been so desperate to be wanted, so afraid of being alone. She'd been harboring the honey-I'm-home dream so long that she'd looked at every man who showed even the slightest bit of potential and cast him in the role of husband. Sad, but true.

Furthermore, she'd met every ex-fiancé through work and each one had been initially interested in her as a result of business-related issues. What her company could do for them. Vince had installed her computer network and Roger had wanted her business account.

In the end, neither one of them had wanted to be her husband.

Curiously, the one man who sparked a blaze of interest was the one man whom she hadn't considered for the role. And she wouldn't consider him now either, she decided firmly. Delaney had jumped to conclusions in the past, had lead with her heart and blindly followed.

Still, she couldn't help but wonder what sort of partner he would make, couldn't help imagining them plundering estate sales together and cuddling in front of the TV on cold winter nights. Couldn't help but fantasize about the rowdy family he clearly loved. Would that she could be a part of something like that, Delaney thought wistfully. Furthermore, despite mental warnings to the contrary, she couldn't help but wonder what sort of parent he'd be. Couldn't help imagining waking up to him every morning…as she had this morning.

Delaney loaded her sponge with moisturizing bath gel and quietly considered that perfect moment. There'd been something altogether different about waking up in his arms this morning, she decided.

Aside from the fact that she was naked—a biggie for her because she'd never slept in the buff in her life, much less with a man beside her—there had still been an intangible, metaphysical something that had kindled between them. She'd awoken with a hard wall of warm male flesh at her back, a hairy leg pressed intimately between her thighs, and a hot hand upon her breast. Warmth eddied through her and sheer delight bloomed in her chest.

Sam, for all intents and purposes, appeared to just want *her*, didn't seem to be remotely interested in anything she or her company might be able to do for him. Dare she consider anything more permanent with him? Dare she see him again beyond this weekend?

Delaney bit her lip and pondered the weighty question. She'd planned to give herself this weekend with him, then cut all ties once they returned to Memphis. The mere idea pricked her heart with regret. She'd planned to essentially use him to help herself rise above her insecurities, had planned to forget him, but remember everything he'd done to her.

Was that even possible? she wondered now. The two were so hopelessly intertwined, she didn't know where the one began and other ended.

Just like her tangled feelings. A part of her wanted to keep things on a safe, unemotional level, enjoy her newfound sensuality without any sticky, complicated hang-ups. Fun, sex, more fun, more sex. Did she mention more sex?

But another part desperately wanted something more permanent. For instance, she wanted exclusive rights to that magnificent body. Didn't want him to think about any woman but herself, much less touch one. She wanted him to keep looking at her the way he did now when he thought she wasn't paying attention—like she was the next best thing since sliced bread. Like he adored her. She swallowed tightly.

Like…he loved her.

Delaney shook herself, angrily soaped her body. Clearly her imagination had run amok again, imagining affection where none existed. He couldn't be in love with her, no more than she could be in love with him. It was ludicrous. They'd known each other less than a week, for pity's sake. They couldn't possibly be in love. They were in serious like, serious lust.

But love?

The vaguest wriggle of…something…shifted significantly in her chest, but she squelched the sentiment determinedly. She knew this road well—it lead directly to Heartache Boulevard, a one-way, dead-end street.

And it was sheer hell getting turned around.

That's why she'd sworn off men. That's why she'd decided they all sucked.

Delaney recognized the futility of that mental tirade and sagged back against the tub. She could not swear off Sam Martelli—she was hopelessly addicted to him—and regrettably, while the rest of his gender might suck, he didn't. Her lips quirked. At least in the derogatory sense, anyway.

Basically, he was all she'd ever wanted and considering no one else would ever suffice, she might as well stick with him and see what happened. Her lips curled wryly. As if she had a choice? As if falling for him hadn't been a foregone conclusion?

Delaney gasped at the thought. *Falling for him?*

Realization settled firmly in her heart, alternately weighting then lightening the traitorous organ.

Oh, hell. She'd fallen for him.

With a wail of frustrated regret and happiness, she sank under the water. *Oh, Lord,* she prayed. *Please let him be the genuine article. Don't let him break my heart.*

"THAT IS POSITIVELY wicked," Sam breathed as Delaney strolled back into the bedroom. *That* being the hot-pink gauzy teddy, matching thong and marabou slippers she currently pirouetted in. Spaghetti straps held up the barely-there sheer baby-doll gown and a single bow tie centered provocatively between her breasts was the only thing that held the racy garment closed.

Sam imagined loosening those ties with his teeth, sliding his hands up and over her slim rib cage and thumbing the undersides of her breasts. Hot-pink marabou fur trimmed the hem and swirled tantalizingly around the tops of her thighs. She bent over the bed, offering him an exaggerated flash of bare-assed beauty, then looked over her shoulder and tossed him a saucy wink.

"I like wicked," she told him. Her eyes flashed meaningfully. "Particularly with you."

He could take her right there, Sam thought, as he fired away several succinct shots with his camera. Move that thong over a mere inch and slide right into her tight heat.

When he'd walked into their room this evening, she'd been waiting for him. Not naked as she'd promised, but almost better than naked, if there were such a thing. He'd found her sitting in the chaise with a sketchbook in her lap, wearing the most lust-provoking outfit he'd ever seen. She'd worn a black silk bustier, matching undies and fishnet stockings held up by a tiny garter belt. For inspiration, she'd told him when he'd stood and stared mutely at her for interminable minutes.

He couldn't argue that the outfit was…*inspiring.*

He'd damn sure been inspired—inspired to take it off of her. Inspired to snap a few pictures of her. A few had led to many, and now they were working on outfit number three. She'd gone from being a timid little kitten in front of the camera to a confident hellcat in under a week. The transformation was damned astounding. The camera loved her, and she moved in front of it better than any woman he'd ever worked with. After a moment, he said as much.

"You're a natural," he told her. "Utterly incredible."

There'd been something different about her tonight, Sam thought consideringly, some indefinable something. She seemed less guarded, more open. Hopeful even, for lack of a better term. Progress, he realized with a pleased start, noting the warm affectionate gleam beneath that brazen sparkle.

Delaney rubbed sinuously against the bedpost and gave him another tempting smile. His heart slammed against his rib cage. "Who wouldn't be for you? I don't think that I've told you yet, but I loved my boudoir photos. You're extremely talented." She lay down on the bed and pretended to smooth away a nonexistent wrinkle from her hose. She cast him a sidelong glance, chuckled softly. "In fact, I'd even considered offering you a job at the *Chifferobe*."

"Is that right?" Sam said lightly as everything inside him mentally leapt at the possibility. He abandoned the idea of working for her when he'd realized that she was The One, had been sure that she'd find some sort of ulterior motive in his interest if she ever learned that he'd submitted his portfolio for her review. That's why he'd pulled it. Clearly, though, that wasn't the case, otherwise she'd have never brought it up.

Sam felt his lips slide into a hesitant grin. He'd been waiting for this opportunity, waiting for her to notice his talent. But it was almost too much to hope for, that he'd get the dream girl *and* the dream job.

"That's right," she confirmed.

Sam paused and scratched his temple, offered her a tentative smile. "You know, it's funny you should say that…because, as it happens, my portfolio sat at the *Chifferobe* for several months."

She stilled, and the instant she looked at him, Sam knew that he'd just made an incredibly stupid tactical error.

"Your portfolio's with my company?" she asked in a curiously flat yet significant tone.

Sam stilled, too, afraid to make any sudden moves. "Er…yes. It was."

Her face became a pale emotionless mask, then she abruptly sat up, looked heavenward and smirked, a grim, pain-filled I-should-have-known expression that immediately turned Sam's insides to lead.

When she finally turned to look at him, the rest of his body turned to lead as well. Her eyes glittered with fury and unshed tears. "We've spent the last five days together and yet you never thought that it was important enough to mention?" She smiled without humor. "Let me guess. Waiting for the right moment?"

Sam swallowed. Panic had made his brain sluggish, and he couldn't get a single syllable past his lips. He opened his mouth, but apparently not fast enough, because Delaney quickly slid from the bed and began to stuff her things into her bag.

"You know what?" she said briskly. "Just save it. Forget I asked that question." She laughed bitterly. "My God, I am such a fool. I know all I need to know."

No, she didn't, dammit, Sam thought as his heart geared into overdrive. She didn't know that he loved her, didn't know that he couldn't live without her. His hands shook at his sides. "No, that's not true. You're not listening. I pulled the damned—"

Another choked laugh pushed from her throat. "You know, Sam, this is an all-too-familiar scene for me and I'd just as soon not play it out."

Sam resisted the urge to tear out his hair. How in God's name had he gotten himself into this mess? He'd barely said a word and yet the few that he'd uttered were clearly the wrong ones. He swallowed tightly. "Delaney, just listen to me a minute," Sam pleaded quietly. "If you'll just let me—"

Delaney held up a hand. "Sam, I mean it. Save it." She paused, dragged in a shallow breath and he caught the slight quiver in her chin. "Please."

Sam shoved an impatient hand through his hair. "Dammit. Delaney, just let me explain—"

She swallowed and he could tell that it cost her. "I think that you've said enough, and I'd really like you to leave me alone and just let me pack." She blew out a shuddering breath. "I w-want to go home."

It was useless, Sam thought numbly as he watched her quietly gather her things. He'd blown it. Pain clogged his throat and he tried to think of some way to make things right. To fix them. But that would want a great deal more time than he had at present. Besides, she wasn't in any frame of mind to listen to anything he had to say. She hadn't heard anything past him telling her that his portfolio had sat at her company for months. Past tense, but she hadn't noticed. Wouldn't listen. He needed to pull back and regroup.

Sam eventually sighed. "If you want to go home, I'll take you home," he offered. "It'll only take—"

"No," she said, clearly losing the battle with patience. Her voice vibrated with tension, with hurt. "I don't want you to take me home. I'll drive myself. The best thing that you can do for me, Mr. Martelli, is to leave me alone." Her voice was final, emphatic.

Sam's chest constricted painfully and he felt every bit of the blood drain from his head as her tone and what it meant fully registered.

"Delaney, please," he pleaded, dangerously close to what felt horrifyingly like... The back of his throat burned, his eyes stung. The top of his head felt like it was about to blow off.

"Go!" she screamed, then her face crumpled pitifully. "Just go."

With a helpless shrug, Sam turned and walked silently from the room. Unable to help himself, he paused at the door and turned back to face her. He let every bit of what he was feeling show in his face. Didn't try to hide a single emotion, including the love and pain. Leaving her felt like an amputation, like he was leaving a part of himself. And he was, Sam realized—his heart.

"You've got it all wrong, you know," he said softly, then just as quietly let himself out.

Delaney's anguished sob followed him down the hall.

14

"ARE YOU OKAY, BOSS?" Beth asked tentatively and carefully handed Delaney the packet of pictures she'd just picked up from the one-hour photo shop. Her assistant was treating her like an unstable bomb again, Delaney thought wearily, speaking softly with no sudden moves, obviously scared that she'd go off.

The effort was moot. Delaney was numb inside, completely without feeling. She didn't possess the necessary spark to go off. Didn't have the energy, the drive required to pull a Katie-kaboom.

"I'm fine, thanks," Delaney said listlessly.

Beth's brow furrowed with concern. "Can I get you anything? A Big Block maybe, or a chocolate volcano from Dibley's?"

She should have been tempted, yet she wasn't. Incredibly, even chocolate therapy hadn't been effective. Delaney shook her head. "No, thanks."

"If you're sure..." Beth said, lingering helplessly.

Delaney swallowed a small breath and met Beth's worried gaze. "I'm sure, Beth. But I appreciate the offer."

Beth bit her bottom lip. "Okay," she sighed. "I'll be right outside should you need anything."

Delaney nodded her thanks, calmly waited on Beth to close the door behind her before she allowed herself to open the deceptively innocuous packet. Her fingers shook as she pulled the stack of photos out and her throat grew tight with unshed emotion as she stared at Sam's irritatingly endearing self-conscious expression. The look was completely at odds with that made-for-sin gloriously naked body. She studied him, traced the achingly familiar curves of his face with her gaze. Those slumberous dark eyes, the angular slant of his jaw, and those oh-so-wonderful lips.

Her eyes burned and a lump formed in her throat and, to her immeasurable irritation, need swiveled low in her belly, a painful reminder of all they'd shared and would never share again.

She flipped through the pictures in quick succession, watched those incredibly gorgeous eyes go from extreme discomfort to downright smoldering in a matter of frames. That hot gaze had been locked on hers, even as one hand idly stroked that impressive staff between his thighs. She'd never seen anything so damned erotic in her life, and just looking at him now brought the entire arousing experience back into sharp focus, made her breath hitch and her nipples bud. Her thighs quiver and her sex wet.

It didn't matter that he'd turned out to be just like everyone else—just another man who'd wanted something from her. Didn't matter that he'd had an ulterior motive—she still wanted him. Desperately.

The wanting she could rationalize—she'd become addicted to him over the past week and her body was simply going into withdrawal. And why wouldn't it? He'd made her blood sing in her veins, made her heart light, made her want to share the same air with him, the same space. It was a wholly natural, albeit miserable, experience, but one that she could easily understand and ultimately forgive.

But what filled her with self-disgust—what she couldn't forgive—was how she desperately wanted to give him the benefit of the doubt, wanted to paint him with a different brush...just so that she could give herself permission to have him back.

Because she wanted him back more than anything.

How screwed up was that?

It didn't matter that he wanted a job, didn't matter that he wasn't any different from any of the other men she'd dated in that regard, though he'd certainly been a one-of-a-kind in every other area. Disheartening? Yes. But when she weighed the pros and cons, being with him just seemed so much more important than hanging on to her tattered pride. Pride was a cold comforter, wouldn't keep her warm at night, wouldn't make her laugh, wouldn't haunt the estate sales with her and tour old homes. Wouldn't give her a family, wouldn't give her a child.

Good grief, Delaney silently railed. Hadn't she learned anything? Would she never learn? How many times did she have to get her heart trampled before she learned not to give it away? How many times was she going to swallow her pride in order to hang on to a man? Hadn't she eaten it enough? Didn't it leave a bad aftertaste?

Not anymore, Delaney decided, though the decision painfully wrenched her heart. She couldn't do it. No matter how much she wanted to, no matter how much she might want to just say to hell with everything, offer Sam a job, take back up where they left off and see where things went…she just couldn't do it. Doing so would make her an even bigger fool than she was before Vince, before Roger. She had to draw the line at some point and, regrettably, it had to be at this one.

With Sam.

A hot tear slipped down her cheek and she bit her trembling lip in an effort to stem the flow. The pain came from a broken place deep down inside her, a place that affected more than her heart—her fractured soul. Delaney knew that she should just let it go, should do exactly what she'd done the previous two times she'd been disappointed in a man, but somehow this time seemed different—the hurt more intense, more bittersweet. With Vince and Roger, heartache—while she never would have admitted it—had been a foregone conclusion. The potential for disappointment had been there.

Delaney swallowed. But for reasons she didn't understand, she'd expected more out of Sam. She'd really thought that he'd been different, had really thought she'd seen a real flash of genuine affection.

That last look that he gave her right before he walked out the door still haunted her, had plagued her all the way back from North Carolina. He'd looked crushed and confused, hurt and wounded. For one agonizing second, she'd wondered if perhaps she'd read things wrong, had somehow made a mistake.

But ultimately, she'd berated herself and deemed it wishful thinking. Fool me once, shame on you. *Fool me twice, shame on me.* She'd known better than to trust her judgment, had known that she was making a terrible mistake, but she hadn't been able to help herself. He'd smiled that come-hither smile and the promise to sin had lurked in his heavy-lidded gaze and something about him allowed her to be the kind of woman she wanted to be. She'd lost her inhibitions, her insecurities, had felt more vibrant and alive in this past week with him than she had in... Well, ever. He turned her on in more ways than one.

While their relationship had ended in disaster, she couldn't regret it. She'd learned that she was capable of being the kind of woman she wanted to be, had learned that she could be sexy and uninhibited, that she didn't have to be ashamed of her body. Granted, she knew she'd never find that kind of freedom with another man—only him—but at least she knew she held the propensity for sensual behavior, knew that she wasn't limited to simply designing her lingerie.

If she'd learned nothing else, that alone had made the whole experience worthwhile. True, she might have a broken heart, but she'd gained self-confidence and self-awareness. Her lips curled with watery humor. There was something to be said for that, anyway.

Beth knocked lightly at the door, then poked her head in. "I've got a couple of things for you to look over," she said.

Delaney drew in a bolstering breath, dabbed her eyes and hastily slipped the photos back into the envelope. She cleared her throat. "Sure."

"Okay," Beth said as she made her way across the carpet. She handed over a folder for Delaney's inspection. "This is the new copy for the *Inspiration* line." Delaney perused the copy, instructed her to make a couple of changes, then nodded her approval. Done with that piece of business, Beth handed her a slim folder. "This guy called last—" she checked the Post-it note attached to the front of the book "—Wednesday morning and asked to withdraw his portfolio. I figured you'd want to have a look at it before I sent it back." She shrugged optimistically. "It's really good."

The fine hairs on Delaney's arms stood on end and her stomach churned as she accepted the folder. She opened the first page, wouldn't have had to look at the name accompanying the work, to know that it belonged to none other than Sam Martelli.

Delaney swallowed tightly. "He wants to w-withdraw his portfolio?" she asked, an unnecessary confirmation. She'd heard Beth correctly.

Beth nodded. "Yeah," she said, her brow drawing

into a puzzled frown. "It was the oddest thing. He was adamant that I return it at once, but I knew that you'd want to see it first, so I held on to it. Should I send it back?"

Delaney's mind spun. Her mouth parched. "Er…when did you say that he called and asked to have it withdrawn?"

"Wednesday morning."

Wednesday morning, Delaney thought faintly. But… Her heart skipped a beat and the air in her lungs thinned, forcing her to drag in short, unsteady breaths. If he called on Wednesday morning, then that meant he'd called and made the request *before* he came to see her. Before he'd asked her to go to Martindale.

Before she'd fallen in love with him.

Blood buzzed in her ears. Why had he done that? Delaney wondered as a hopeful explanation sprouted in her breast. If he'd wanted a job with her company, then why had he called and withdrawn his portfolio after meeting her? After making the connection? Her head gave an imperceptible shake and a curious winging sensation commenced in her chest. It didn't make any logical sense…but she'd never been good at thinking logically anyway. Her thoughts tended to run to the illogical and she illogically hoped that she wasn't reading too much into this revelation.

For instance, she illogically hoped that he'd pulled his portfolio because he wanted *her* and not just a job with her company. Illogically hoped that he'd pulled it because he didn't want her finding out about it later and then jumping to the wrong conclusion.

Which was exactly what she'd done, Delaney realized with a sickening start. She'd heard the one sentence about his portfolio, then completely refused to listen to any explanation. She'd cut him off at the knees, had cloaked herself in anger, and hadn't let him say more than a handful of words. Hadn't been able to see past the immediate hurt.

What had he said? *You've got it all wrong, you know.*

Oh, God.

And she hadn't believed him.

Nervous tension suddenly vibrated her spine and she shot up from her chair, grabbed the portfolio, the packet of pictures and her purse. "I'll see to this," Delaney said in a somewhat strangled voice and strode briskly for the door. "I'm gone for the day."

"O-okay," Beth said, clearly dumbfounded at her boss' erratic behavior.

You've got it all wrong, you know, Delaney thought again, remembering his bleak, hurt expression. She didn't know whether that was true or not, but she was grimly determined to find out.

And illogically…she hoped she had.

SAM SLOWLY PULLED UP IN front of Delaney's house and stared at her front door. Anxiety balled in his gut and tension settled in his backbone. Back again, with no plan, Sam thought, his lips curling into the shadow of a smile.

It had only been a couple of days since he'd seen her and yet it felt like forever. Like a damned eternity. He missed her terribly, missed the damn "quickening" and all the maddening sensations that went with it. The gooseflesh, the tingling scalp, the whirling behind his navel. He missed all of it. Since she'd left Saturday night—she'd rented a car to make the return trip—he'd felt disconnected from himself, curiously numb. Pre-Delaney, he'd come to call it. Pre-life.

Sam had decided when Delaney left Saturday night to give her a little space, to let her calm down and rationally consider what had happened between them. He'd known that if she didn't come to realize he was different on her own—if she didn't make the distinction—then he'd ultimately pay the price. He would constantly be paying for the sins of others, and dammit, that just wasn't fair.

He wanted her to realize that he wasn't like every other guy, and figured if he left her alone long enough, she would eventually reach that conclusion on her own, without any prodding on his part. She'd see past her pain, past her anger and would eventually discover that what they'd had was special, couldn't be recreated, that ultimately *he* was different from all those other losers she'd previously been involved with. Bastards who weren't good enough for her, Sam thought viciously. Bastards who'd used her to further themselves.

But that confidence had begun to rapidly deteriorate with each passing second he didn't hear from her. What if she didn't realize what they had was special? What if she didn't realize that, while he might have gone into her shoot with a business-related ulterior motive, he'd come out of it with a personal one—to have her?

Sam couldn't stand it any longer. He'd had to see her. He'd called her office and her assistant had told him that she'd left for the day. He'd assumed she'd be at home, yet her car was absent from her driveway. No matter. He'd wait it out. She had to come home sometime, right? When she did, he'd be waiting…provided Mrs. Carter—the pit bull in support hose, Delaney had called her—didn't call her son, Sam thought as he caught her glaring at him from over the privet hedge.

Sam smiled and waved at her, then laughed when she immediately scowled and retreated hurriedly into her house.

Five minutes later a police cruiser pulled in behind his Tahoe. Sam swore, saw Mrs. Carter's curtains twitch. A couple of minutes passed, then a large officer who looked like he'd been weaned on steroids exited the cruiser, sauntered up and tapped on Sam's glass.

Sam pasted on a smile free of irritation—no small

feat when he literally seethed with it—and lowered the window. "Yes, sir?"

"Is there any particular reason you are parked here on this street?"

"I'm waiting for Ms. Walker," Sam replied amiably. This guy could rip him limb from limb were he so inclined. He looked like a damned sasquatch.

"How long have you been here?"

Sam tapped the steering wheel, pretended to think about it. "Around thirty minutes."

"He's lying!" Mrs. Carter, who'd escaped his notice and who'd apparently come to join in the interrogation, said with a sniff. "He's been here an hour, at least."

Sam bared his teeth in a semblance of a smile. "That might be more accurate, however, last time I checked waiting wasn't against the law."

Mrs. Carter's eyes flashed, then she turned a determined expression up at the officer. "Make him leave, son," she ordered. "Delaney has had enough to deal with lately—she doesn't need another one of these kooks plaguing her today."

"I'm not a kook," Sam insisted, vaguely recalling Delaney mentioning something to the same effect the first time he'd visited her house. He'd been so overwrought and out of sorts, he hadn't been able to think clearly. "I'm a friend."

"No, you're not, sonny. You're a kook," she insisted. "If you were a friend, then you'd know to come when she was at home." She bobbed her head.

"Now move on. She doesn't give interviews from her home. Not to any of the papers, not for possible employment." Her eyes narrowed. "Not for anything." She blew out a disgusted breath. "For pity's sake, show some respect. Make an appointment—don't bother her at home."

Guilt pricked at the reminder that he too been one of those people who wanted something from her, and he truly understood why she'd be wary of anyone whom she suspected of an ulterior motive. But he hadn't shown up at her house like one of the kooks, as Mrs. Carter had so eloquently put it. He'd sent his portfolio to her office and when he'd realized that their relationship was destined for something more, he'd pulled the damn thing. He was different, dammit. He wasn't Roger, he wasn't any other guy.

He was different. He had to prove it to her.

But if Officer Testosterone had anything to say about it, he wasn't going to get the chance.

"I'm afraid I'm going to have to ask you to leave," the officer said, much to Sam's immense displeasure. He needed to see her now, more than ever.

"Look," Sam said, striving for a calm he didn't feel. "I'm not hurting anyone, I'm not breaking the law. I'm simply waiting on a friend. That's all."

The officer's big chest swelled as he drew in a self-important breath. "I would hate for this to get ugly. I've told you to leave. We can do this one of two ways, you can go willingly—or unwillingly—

but one way or the other, you will be going.'' He cracked his knuckles. ''Understand?''

''That's telling him, John,'' Mrs. Carter said with a succinct self-righteous nod.

Oh, hell, Sam thought as irritation twisted his insides into a huge seething knot. He couldn't blame her for coming to Delaney's defense—was glad that she did. He just wished that she'd nabbed a genuine kook—not him.

''Listen—''

''Okay. I warned you,'' the officer said, then promptly opened Sam's door and started to forcibly drag him out of the car. Sam instinctively resisted, outraged at the man's gall. ''Dammit, I haven't done anything wrong!''

In short order Sam found himself flattened against the car, his arm wrenched up behind his back. He winced.

''Hey!'' a familiar outraged voice screamed. ''John, what the hell are you doing? Mrs. Carter, what's going on?''

Sam tried to turn toward the sound of Delaney's voice, but John had him in a death grip. He heard the sharp rap of her heels across the pavement drawing closer, then, ''I said what the hell are you doing?'' she repeated. ''Let him go.''

''Do you know this man, Delaney?'' John asked.

''He's been lurking in his car,'' Mrs. Carter shared knowingly. ''Waiting for you to get home.''

Delaney huffed an exasperated breath. ''Yes, I

know him. He's a friend. Now for heaven's sake, let him go.''

"If you're sure," John hedged, clearly disappointed that he hadn't been able to twist Sam's arm clean out of the socket.

"I'm sure," Delaney told him, her voice tight.

John reluctantly lowered Sam's arm and stepped back, allowing Sam to finally turn around and meet Delaney's tense gaze. To his vast relief, goose bumps peppered his skin and his scalp prickled with awareness. That curious whirling behind his navel started again, sucking the very air from his lungs with its intensity. He wanted to hug her more than anything, wanted to breathe in her sweet scent, feel that soft womanly body against his. The urge almost brought him to his knees, yet he resisted. He had a lot more riding on this than a mere hug and he instinctively knew the time wasn't right.

"I didn't mean to sic John on your friend, Delaney," Mrs. Carter said with a regretful sniff, her voice contrite. "I was just trying to look out for you."

Delaney tore her gaze from his and regarded her neighbor with a warm smile. "I know. Thank you."

Seemingly satisfied, Mrs. Carter snagged her gigantic son's arm and herded him efficiently toward her house. "Come along, John. I've got a nice mug of cocoa waiting."

"Sorry," Delaney murmured with a sheepish

quirk of her lips. "She's a little overzealous when it comes to looking out for me."

"It's fine," Sam said, and shoved his hands in his jacket pockets to keep from reaching for her. "No harm done."

"Er..." She cocked her head. "How long have you been waiting?"

"About an hour."

She huffed a short breath, crossed her arms protectively over her chest. "Funny. That's about how long I've been sitting in the parking lot of your apartment building."

Sam's senses heightened. "You have?"

She wore a curiously guarded, yet hopeful expression that made something near his heart shift. "Yeah," she told him. "I'd decided to come home and try to call, try to catch up with you that way."

"I'm eternally grateful." His conjured a wry smile. "I'd undoubtedly be on my way to 201 Poplar if you hadn't made such a timely appearance."

Her eyes twinkled. "You know the address of the police department?"

Sam shrugged. "I make a yearly donation to the Widowed Officers Fund. It's easy to remember."

Seemingly impressed, her gaze softened and she gestured toward her house. "Would you like to come in?"

Sam nodded, heartened by the invitation and followed her inside. She shrugged out of her coat and hung it on the hall tree. Following her lead, Sam did the same.

A tense beat elapsed, then slid into five as they stood awkwardly in her foyer and stared at one another. They both swallowed, then...

"I owe you—"

"I'm sorry—"

They shared a laugh and, thankfully, that seemed to lighten the moment.

"Sorry," Sam said. "You go first."

Delaney pushed a hand through her hair, her lips curled into an endearingly nervous smile. "Thank you. I'd like to go first because one, I owe you an apology and, secondly, I have a question for you." She took a deep breath, for courage, he supposed. "I, uh...I'm sorry for the way that I acted in Martindale. I should have let you explain, but I was so mad and I couldn't get past that anger and I just—" she gestured wildly "—blew up." She cast him a woeful glance. "I'm truly sorry."

Something in Sam's chest lightened, swelled with hope. "Apology accepted."

"Now for the question." Her eyes searched his and the torturous emotion he read in those gorgeous green depths unwittingly propelled his feet toward her. "Why did you pull your portfolio from the *Chifferobe?*" she asked softly, and he could tell that his answer was incredibly important to her. She seemed to be holding her breath, silently praying for him to say the right thing.

Sam lovingly traced her face with his gaze. "Because I knew the first moment that I saw you that you were the one for me," Sam replied with complete honesty, "and I didn't want to give you any reason to suspect an ulterior motive. Not one." Sam paused, let the sincerity of his words sink in. "I won't lie to you, Delaney. I was initially thrilled that you'd booked your appointment. I wanted to use your boudoir photos to showcase my talent, wanted you to look at my portfolio and give me a shot at your magazine. There are so many ways I can see to make it better, so many—" Sam drew up short, momentarily derailed by his enthusiasm. He offered her a small smile. "Any photographer worth his salt would want to work for you." Sam took another step forward and smoothed his fingers down the side of one heartbreakingly beautiful cheek. "But my motives took a drastic change after I saw you. Working for you no longer mattered...I wanted you. Just you," he told her, his voice soft yet fierce with emotion. "Am I making myself clear?"

A sigh stuttered past her lips and her eyes welled with tears. Another hopeful smile trembled on her lips. "Would you have ever mentioned it if I hadn't?"

"No. I knew you'd assume the worst and draw the wrong conclusion."

"And that's what I did," she said miserably. "I assumed the worst of you, when you didn't deserve it. I'm so sorry. I've just made so many wrong decisions, made so many mistakes. I wanted to believe the best about you, I really did…but I just couldn't trust my own judgment.''

Sam shrugged lightly. "It's understandable." He tipped her chin up and gazed meaningfully in her achingly familiar face. "But you can trust mine. You can trust me. I swear it."

He shivered violently as a particularly intense rush of Martelli energy coursed through him.

Her brow furrowed. "You're shivering again. Do I need to turn up the heat?" she asked, concerned.

Sam shook his head. While they were making confessions, he might as well make another one. He chuckled. "I'm not the least bit cold—can't be around you." He placed her hand against his neck, causing another wave of gooseflesh to break out over his body. "Feel? I'm burning up. Have been since I met you."

"Then why do you have chills all the time?" Her eyes widened in fear. "My God. Are you— Are you sick?"

"No," he quickly reassured. "It's more bizarre than that."

"Then what?"

He smiled, feeling ridiculous. "It's called the Martelli 'quickening.'"

Predictably, she arched a skeptical brow. "A what?"

Sam quickly explained the Martelli phenomenon, and thanked God that, while she did appear quite shocked, she hadn't immediately withdrawn from his embrace and called Officer Testosterone back.

She drew back and stared at him. "Let me get this straight? This Martelli 'quickening' lets you know when you find the right woman?"

"Right."

"And you 'quickened,' or whatever, when you first saw me? You knew I was the one for you? That we'd fall in love and be together forever. Like all of your ancestors have? I'm your she-wolf?"

He felt his eyes crinkle at the corners. "Correct."

Her eyes widened in outrage. "Then why the hell didn't you tell me?" she all but screamed. She whacked him on the chest. "You could have saved us a great deal of heartache if you'd just told me."

Sam blinked, astounded. "What? You'd have thought I was a damned nut. What was I supposed to say? Excuse me, Ms. Walker, but according to my goosebumps, you and I are destined to fall in love and spend the rest of our lives together?"

She winced adorably, mulled it over. "Well... there is that."

Sam felt his gaze soften as he looked down at her. He brushed his lips across hers. "There is that," he repeated. Then he deepened the kiss, put every ounce of feeling that he possessed into the mating of their mouths. Made love to her mouth the way he wanted to make love to her body. Need vibrated through him and he'd hardened to the point of pain. God, he had to have her.

Right now.

She drew back and stared drunkenly up at him. Happiness shimmered in her bright gaze and a wicked edge turned her smile. "And *there is that*," she murmured meaningfully, rubbing her pearled nipples against his chest. "Let's take *that* upstairs, why don't we?"

Sam peeled her sweater over her head and latched his mouth onto her breast through the fabric of her bra. "Let's don't and say we did."

She laughed, arched her back, pushing her needy nipple farther into his mouth. Her breath hitched. "Sounds like a good plan."

"I've been fantasizing about this table," Sam told her as he swiftly removed every stitch of her clothing. He sat her on top of the antique refectory table.

Delaney's small hands worked just as efficiently, his clothes joining hers in the discarded pile on the floor. She wrapped her hand around his rod and quickly guided him to her hot, wet center. Sam gritted his teeth against the exquisite sensation, then slid into her with one smooth stroke.

Home, he thought.

She instantly convulsed around him, bit his shoulder, then arched her neck back and reveled in the feel of their joined bodies as he sank repeatedly into her welcoming flesh.

"I love you," Sam said brokenly between thrusts, pushing her further and further toward release. "You got that part, right?"

She fisted around him, came hard. Delaney's lids fluttered shut and her mouth formed a silent *O* of pleasure. "I g-got it," she screamed in an orgasmic rush. "I l-love you, too."

Hearing those words sparked the most extraordinary sensation Sam had ever felt. His entire body tautened in awe of a cataclysmic eruption. Every cell in his body sharpened, his skin prickled from head to toe and the most incredible, breath-robbing, thought-shattering orgasm blasted from his loins.

A long, slow howl issued from his throat, then he groaned and collapsed against her, almost unable to hold up his own weight. He trembled from the force of it, shook uncontrollably and knew that what had just happened had inexplicably bound them together forever.

Chest heaving, Sam said, "That's the s-second time we've made love without protection. I h-hope you aren't opposed to starting a family i-immediately." For reason's that escaped him, he had the inexplicable premonition that they'd just done exactly that.

That sounded like sheer heaven, Delaney thought. The idea of carrying his child warmed her from the inside out. "I'm not opposed at all," she told him, flexing her feminine muscles around him, listening as his breath caught in his throat and watching his eyes all but roll back in his head.

God, she loved this man.

"In fact, I'm quite in favor of the idea." She

leaned forward, framed his face with her hands and planted a long, hungry kiss on his lips. Hers, she thought as he throbbed deep inside her. He had been different…and he was all hers. Not just for today, or for tomorrow or in the meantime—forever. Her senses soared.

"Is th-that right?" Sam asked brokenly.

"That's right." Delaney chuckled wickedly and her heart began to beat in tune with the Wedding March. "Inseminate me again, baby."

Oh, would he ever, Sam thought, then swiftly turned the thought into a reality.

Epilogue

"HE'S FALLEN ASLEEP," Delaney whispered softy. "I need to lay him down." She smoothed her fingers over her son's dark, downy head and her chest inexplicably filled with wondrous joy.

"Hold on just another minute," Sam told her haltingly, face behind the camera. "This is too good. I can't—I can't stop. Just a few more minutes."

Though her heart filled with exasperated happiness, Delaney resisted the urge to roll her eyes. He'd been pleading *a few more minutes* for the past hour. For the past year. Her shutterbug husband had been taking pictures of her for what felt like forever. Racy photos, then when she'd become pregnant, he'd become almost obsessed with her maternal form, wanted to catalogue every change in her body.

Her pregnancy had inspired a new line of maternity lingerie at the *Chifferobe* and her new senior photographer, a hot guy by the name of Sam Martelli, had headed up the project as well as fine-tuned others. Together they were an unbeatable team. Her business had enjoyed success before he came onboard, but now *Laney's Chifferobe* was a force to be reckoned with. They gotten married immediately after getting back together and the speedy wedding had sparked a flurry of controversial publicity in Memphis. The *Herald,* in particular, had taken an unfavorable slant to her marriage. But one visit from Sam, his attorney, father and brothers in tow, had nixed any further uncharitable articles.

She'd thought that his fascination with taking pictures of her would wane once the baby was born, thought her son would become his new favorite subject, but she'd been wrong. Oh, he'd taken thousands of pictures of their baby, but had taken thousands more of she and the baby together. Nudes, stills, indoor, outdoor, everywhere.

She'd come to the baby's room to nurse, had sat down in the rocker in front of the window and, when her greedy son had latched on to her breast, contentment and happiness had permeated her every pore. The rightness of the moment—of her life with Sam and her child—had hit her. Sam had chosen that exact moment to walk into the room, he'd gotten that look, hurried off, then reappeared with his camera. Delaney's lips curled. Sam Jr. had finished his morning snack thirty minutes ago, and yet Sam Sr. still wouldn't let her get up.

Delaney heaved a small sigh. "Sam, I'm going to lay him down. I'm getting up now."

"But—"

"But nothing."

"Oh, all right." He set the camera aside, met her at the crib and nudged a blanket out of the way so that she could lay the baby down. "God, he's perfect, Delaney," Sam murmured softly, reverently. Though he wasn't comfortable with it yet, her big, tough, Italian husband had been known to tear up over their baby.

A smile gently tugged her lips. That was an assessment she wholeheartedly agreed with. "He's like his daddy," Delaney told him.

Sam slid his arm about her waist and pulled her close. "Nah, he's definitely like his momma." He bent down and kissed her nose.

"I suppose we could share the credit," Delaney replied drolly as familiar warmth started at her toes and fizzed to her hairline.

"There is that." Sam drew back and inclined his head. Something hot and wicked lurked in his dark-as-sin gaze, clung to that lazy smile. "When are Pops and the clan supposed to be here?"

She knew where this line of questioning was headed. Anticipation drew a slow smile across her lips. "They're coming for lunch. Not for several more hours." She hadn't simply acquired a husband, she'd gotten a family to boot. A big, loud family whom she absolutely adored.

Sam bent down and nuzzled her neck. He hummed under his breath. "I don't know about you, but I'm hungry now." He nipped at her earlobe, sending a shock of gooseflesh across her skin.

Delaney shuddered delicately as pleasure hummed

through her. "Yeah?" she murmured. "I could go for something."

"Yeah? For what?"

Delaney slid her fingers into the hair at his nape, dragged him down and kissed him until she could scarcely draw a breath, until she felt him prod against her belly. She laced her fingers through his and tugged him toward their bedroom. Her eyes twinkled. "Chocolate-covered sex."

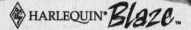

Blaze

HARLEQUIN® Blaze™

In L.A., nothing remains confidential for long…

KISS & TELL

Don't miss

Tori Carrington's

exciting new miniseries featuring four
twentysomething friends—
and the secrets they *don't* keep.

Look for:

#105—NIGHT FEVER
October 2003

#109—FLAVOR OF THE MONTH
November 2003

#113—JUST BETWEEN US…
December 2003

Available wherever Harlequin books are sold.

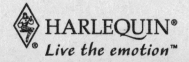

HARLEQUIN®
Live the emotion™

Visit us at www.eHarlequin.com

HARLEQUIN®

Temptation

THE WRONG BED

What happens when a girl finds herself in the
wrong bed...with the *right* guy?

Find out in:

#866 NAUGHTY BY NATURE by Jule McBride
February 2002

#870 SOMETHING WILD by Toni Blake
March 2002

#874 CARRIED AWAY by Donna Kauffman
April 2002

#878 HER PERFECT STRANGER by Jill Shalvis
May 2002

#882 BARELY MISTAKEN by Jennifer LaBrecque
June 2002

#886 TWO TO TANGLE by Leslie Kelly
July 2002

Midnight mix-ups have never been so much fun!

HARLEQUIN®
Makes any time special ®

Visit us at www.eHarlequin.com

HTNBN2

If you enjoyed what you just read,
then we've got an offer you can't resist!

Take 2 bestselling
love stories FREE!
Plus get a FREE surprise gift!

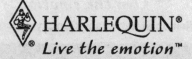

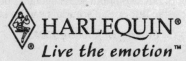